Also by José J. Veiga

The Misplaced Machine and Other Stories (1970)

THIS IS A BORZOI BOOK PUBLISHED IN
NEW YORK BY ALFRED A. KNOPF

THE THREE TRIALS
OF MANIREMA

THE THREE TRIALS
OF MANIREMA

 By José J. Veiga

Translated from the
Portuguese by Pamela G. Bird

ALFRED A. KNOPF 1970 New York

To CLERIDA, with love

Translator's Note

THE HOUSES in the interior towns of Brazil were nearly always divided up the middle by a passageway that ran from the front door to the comparatively large kitchen, where the family ate their meals. On the right of the passageway was a parlor and perhaps a bedroom, on the left one or two bedrooms, then the wide kitchen and a door that opened onto a yard where the sanitary facilities were, and some chickens and a few bushes or trees. Many of the houses had a garden behind that, with fruit trees, vegetables, a cow or a goat, more poultry. In front there was a porch, as wide as the house. If the front door opened onto the street, the indispensable porch was at the side or the back. The few windows had no glass—they were made with wooden shutters, opening outward. The interior walls often did not go right up to the high ceiling, for the sake of coolness. Water was brought in from a spring (towns of any size had a paved fountain where the spring was, but many of the houses had their own wells, and some of the water was carried from a nearby river). It was kept in huge clay jars on a metal stand, a gourd with a handle hanging nearby for dispensing the water for drinking or washing. Laundry was usually done at the edge of rivers or streams, left to bleach on the grass, then rinsed again and hung to dry on fences and bushes. Electricity did not exist—lighting was by candle and kerosene lamp, and cooking on kerosene or wood stoves.

Most of this is still true in many a small interior town today, the only additions being transistor radios, cars, and some packaged products. Cigarettes are still being rolled by hand—paper favored by some smokers, corn husks by others—and filled with rope tobacco that is scraped off with a penknife, then chopped into minute pieces in the palm of the hand.

All married or older unmarried women are addressed by their first name preceded by *Dona*. Men in the hinterland have a *Seu* before either name, which is a contraction of the *Senhor* (Mister) used in the cities. I have not translated christian names or place names unless they are too difficult for English pronunciation.

PAMELA G. BIRD

Bahia, October 1969

Contents

THE ARRIVAL

NIGHT CAME early to Manirema. The sun had barely begun to disappear behind the hills—slipping away without warning—when it was time to light the lamps, bring in the calves, wrap up in shawls. The cold, hiding until then in the riverbeds and caverns and damp cellars, crept silently into the houses like a curious damp-nosed dog.

Manirema at nightfall—worry, warnings, restlessness. Carried on a wind that was playing hide-and-seek around the street corners came the inevitable sounds of barking and the wail of babies afraid of the dark. Deep-voiced opinions of frogs in debate, crickets shrilly sharpening tools, bats stitching the air at random, draping black bunting over the square, decorating it for some mournful celebration. Darkness was coming to Manirema.

The pack train came slowly down the road, almost invisible in the all-embracing blue. Some townsmen, standing on the bridge trying to postpone the night, dimly heard the sigh and creak of leather saddle bags, the flinty sound of horseshoes striking stone. Interest quickened. It might be a load of salt bacon, an item in short supply. While they waited for confirmation—optimists to a man— they lit up cigarettes. The talk was of rising prices, in-

3

creasing shortages, and the terrible taste of beef fat, muck that sticks to the lips and probably gums up the innards as well.

"Even dogs won't eat it. Mine sniffs it and runs."

"That's why we get all these gut aches."

"They say it won't be long before there's no salt. It's already getting scarce in Valdijurnia."

"The day's coming when everything'll be scarce."

"The end of the world is what's coming."

"End of the world? How could the world just end?"

"It could! Whoever made this world can easily put an end to it too."

"Aagh, that's the priests talking to scare you. D'you think whoever made the world went to all that trouble just to unmake it afterward? It's not like it's some kid's toy."

The water went on whispering under the bridge, making little whirlpools around the supports, bubbling and frothing. Chilly drafts of air rose in small waves, carrying the smell of wet sand and musty leaves. Frogs and crickets, competing, took possession of the night. More cigarettes were smoked and the butts tossed into the water, to disappoint the fish. Suddenly someone remembered:

"Where's that pack train?"

"Yeah, that's funny. They didn't go by."

"Think they went back?"

"Back where? It doesn't make sense."

"Maybe it wasn't a pack train . . ."

A silly attempt to dismiss the matter. Hadn't they all

seen—or, anyway, caught a glimpse of—the pack animals stumbling under the weight of the loads, drivers behind, cracking whips?

"What d'you mean, it wasn't a pack train? I even counted the animals—eight or ten of them."

"I counted up to ten and then got mixed up. Probably more."

Ten pack mules disappearing on a straight road that had no detours? Some explanation was called for, a thing like that could not just be ignored.

"You know what I think? We were too hungry for that bacon. When you want to see something so much you end up seeing it in your own head."

"But didn't we all see it? Didn't we count the animals? I wasn't even thinking of bacon."

"Well, maybe it was some animals that got loose and were grazing. They came out of the brush and then they went back."

A weak interpretation, but they let it pass. To reject it meant finding another, and that pack train hadn't disappeared into thin air or floated away on the clouds.

"Yeah, could be. I don't see so good far off and even worse when it's dark."

"Well, now that you mention it, I said I saw 'em because I didn't want to be contrary. What I really saw was some kind of round shapes, I couldn't swear it was a pack train. In the dark any rope is a snake and any priest is a monk."

But there's another saying: a problem buried is a problem sown. Up in the town others had also seen the pack

5

train. Cutting short conversations on sidewalks and street corners, they made for the bridge, to gather around the drivers and find out where the wares were to be sold. The next day they would get up with the dawn and be first at the trough. On their way they ran into the men coming back from the bridge.

"The pack train? Did you see the pack train?"

"It wasn't a pack train."

"Who're you kidding? We saw them from the square. Where'd they go?"

"Search me."

"Didn't you ask?"

"Not me. What do I want with roof tiles?"

"Just roof tiles?"

"Tiles. Adobe bricks. Clay pots."

"No bacon?"

"Didn't see any."

The others pretended to believe it. Quite obviously there was not enough bacon to go around and what there was would be sold on the sly to the highest bidders. The trick was to feign disinterest, get up early in the morning, and track it down. It takes cunning to beat cunning.

Next morning the town awoke to the same bacon shortage, but something new had been added: a great encampment, smoking and pulsing with life, had been set up on the other side of the river. It was such a surprise that people could hardly believe their eyes. They got up, went to the window for a moment before washing their faces—and there it was. They called to one another, pointed,

6

asked questions, but no one knew anything. In every house it was the same: people hurrying into clothes, their arms catching in the sleeves, dashing out with no breakfast, stepping on sleeping dogs, dogs yelping, men cursing, people bumping into each other, hats being knocked off—a real hullabaloo. Everyone must have seen it at the same time; the high part of the square, the second-story windows, the riverbank, all were crowded with townspeople staring, pointing, and arguing.

Could they be gypsies? It didn't look like it. Gypsies put up tents any which way, messily, with things draped all over them; these people camped in a straight line, two even rows properly measured, with a sort of square in the middle. Gypsies don't keep dogs and these people did. You could see them playing in the grass, leaping up and snapping at the air, chasing each other around the tents, wagging their tails, glad to be alive. The men were busy carrying bundles, opening them, consulting with one another, and paying no attention whatever to the town close by. Were they engineers? Mining people? Revenuers?

"Let's go talk to them and find out," someone suggested.

The others thought about it and disagreed.

"We'd better not. If they're stand-offish, we better be too. We don't want to be pushy."

"It could be they're waiting till they get settled, get the ground broken in; then they'll come around and introduce themselves."

"Yeah, that's it. Let's wait. No need to go running to them."

7

Impatiently, Manirema waited. People with windows facing on the camp watched it constantly. If they left their posts at all, it was only for a quick dash to the stove for a hurried swig of scalding coffee right from the pot, then back to the window. No one ate properly; they were all afraid of missing something if they sat down for a moment. Those who did eat stood in front of the window munching, mostly just a slice of sausage or a hunk of meat, eyes never moving from the campsite.

"They're putting up a flagpole. What d'you think it's for?"

"There's a couple wrestling in the grass. D'you think it's a fight?"

"Now they're splashing water on each other."

"I guess they're gonna eat. They're getting in line, holding plates."

By late afternoon the townspeople began to fear that nothing *would* happen. Circles of talkers, formed here and there, became silent at any sound of footsteps or a horse approaching, watchful for signs of possible emissaries. Shopkeepers stayed open late, a courtesy to the strangers in case they needed anything—and also for the good name of Manirema. Just imagine what the men might say if they were unable to buy a bundle of candles or a can of kerosene! The shopkeepers waited a long time, seated on the edges of their counters or on chairs tipped back against the wall.

Manirema went to bed thinking about its peculiar neighbors and making plans for dealing with them when the time came. People who got up in the middle of the night saw the campsite still lit up, shadows busy everywhere.

THE FIRST CONTACT was made by Father Prudente, on his return from some sacred expedition. The priest and his assistant were coming down the road in midmorning, their mules with lowered heads, shading their eyes from the brightness of the sun. Near the bridge they met two men carrying a leather water bag hanging from a pole, each with one end of the pole on his shoulder, the bag in the middle, water leaking from every seam. Accustomed to being treated deferentially on the open road, Father Prudente turned toward them expecting a greeting. They did not even touch their hat brims, something they could easily have done because their hands were free. The priest then greeted them himself, not so much to teach them as not to seem proud. They did not reply; they acted as if they had not heard. The assistant, who lagged some steps behind and clearly witnessed this affront, said "Good morning" loudly and in a challenging tone. The men paid no attention and, almost as if they had rehearsed it, began to whistle a little tune, probably something they had made up. The assistant came up to the priest.

"Did you see that, Monsignor?"

"Yes, Balduino. They don't seem to like us."

Talking about it afterward, Balduino said that he happened to look back just as one of the men made a rude gesture in their direction, shaking his right fist over his head.

9

"The only thing that stopped me from giving those hard-heads a lesson was that I know the monsignor doesn't approve of fighting."

If those men were as obstinate and impudent as Balduino said they were, then Manirema was in for a lot of headaches. It was a good thing no one had gone running to them, or he would have come back with his tail between his legs. And it was going to be awfully funny if the owner of the property came back from his farm unexpectedly and ordered them to clear the site. Because Julio Barbosa was just the man to do it—an honest, upright fellow, but not the sort to trifle with. Seu Julio discouraged familiarity by wiping every trace of a smile off his face when he left his house, and if he said "Good morning" it was more a command than a greeting, so that you spent the rest of the day worried in case you disobeyed. He was quite likely to march into the camp, call for the leader, greet him politely and, without giving him a chance to reply, order the camp-site cleared, turn his back, and leave them gaping. That was what the town was waiting for.

"But what if the men won't go away?"

The doubt was voiced by Balduino, who based it on his earlier experience, but no one wanted to consider it—nothing like this had ever happened before and if it happened now, Julio Barbosa would know how to deal with it.

"They'll go. They have no excuse to stay."

With this certainty, and with the men showing no inclination to meet with them, the townspeople went about their business and behaved as if there were no strangers camped almost on their doorsteps. At night, when they closed their windows before going to bed, they saw the bright lights of the encampment and tried to convince themselves there was really nothing there, remembering the fallow field as it had been before, a bluish clearing in the vast reaches of the country night. The exasperating neighbors and the dangers they might bring were blotted out. Later there would be dreams in which the men of the camp figured as the enemy, but they would be just dreams, powerful only in the darkness of bedrooms, dissipating in the light of day.

However, because they were so near and were doing all kinds of building on Julio Barbosa's property, it was inevitable that the men would come up against someone from town. It happened to Geminiano Dias, the owner of a wagon for hire. Geminiano was carting manure for a vegetable garden and, on one of his trips past the campsite, he was stopped at the fence by a tall man with lantern jaw and crew-cut hair.

"Wanna trade your wagon, fella?"

Geminiano did not like his manner, so he did not stop or pay any attention. The man walked up to the next fence post and repeated:

"Wanna sell your wagon? I'll give you good money."

"No, I don't," answered Geminiano, through clenched teeth.

The man would not give up. He moved up one more fence post and made it sound as if he were giving a command.

11

"Stop a minute, why don't you?"

"I can't. If I could I'd stay home."

The man ducked quickly under the fence, ran a few steps, and stopped in front of the cart.

"Now wait a minute, fella," he said. "When a donkey speaks, another donkey stops to listen."

"I don't understand donkey talk," replied Geminiano. "When I talk to donkeys I talk with this," and he showed the poised whip.

By this time the wagon's donkey had stopped of its own accord. The man stroked its nose, pondering whether to take Geminiano on. He decided against it—anyone sitting higher up, and armed with a whip, has a certain natural advantage.

"Well, 'donkey' is a manner of speaking. It's a saying back where I come from."

"It is here, too."

"You really don't want to sell the wagon?"

"Nope."

"How about renting it?"

"That I'll do. It's my business."

Encouraged, the man took hold of the reins, as if he were going to take over the wagon that very moment.

"Better move. The donkey's skittish," Geminiano warned.

"Skittish? Then it's no good to me. I'll just hire the cart."

"And who's going to pull it?"

"We got our own animals. Good ones."

"I don't work with no other animals. I got Serrote and I don't need any other."

12

"You don't understand. I just want the cart. I don't need the donkey or you."

"It's you that don't understand. When I hire out this wagon, it's just for the one job. I drive it myself, with my own donkey."

"Yeah, but I only need the cart. You can get down and walk the donkey back. Spill the manure over there," said the man, putting his hand on the harness to unhitch it.

"Go chase yourself," snapped Geminiano, slashing at the donkey in his anger and leaving the man looking foolish at the edge of the road.

The story spread quickly and Geminiano was universally praised for knowing how to put the man in his place. Was that any way to do business, the way these strangers talked down to you, grabbing at the reins, and giving orders as if they owned everything? But when the news reached Amancio Mendes' store, Mendes did not agree. Speaking at the top of his lungs, as usual, Amancio made sure he could be heard in the street.

"That nigger is a jerk. Just because he's got himself a wagon he thinks he's somebody. Wait till he hears from me."

It happened that Justino Moreira was in the store and, as buyer of Geminiano's manure, he thought it his duty to defend him.

"But he'd started a job and couldn't just stop in the middle."

Amancio then realized what he had said. He hadn't wanted to affront Justino, a decent man and a friend. That

13

was the trouble with shooting off your mouth when there was no need even to open it. Why did he have to go and open fire on Geminiano and, worse, in defense of those men? But it was too late now, what was said was said. It would mean losing face if he backed out in front of all those people.

"Yeah, but he was wrong. He had no reason to insult the man. If it was me, Geminiano would've got down from that cart in a hurry. I don't take smart-talk from niggers."

Having voiced his opinion, and in front of everyone, Justino felt his duty was done. If he pressed the matter he would be starting a quarrel for no good reason. Amancio was as ready to fight as he was to sneeze; he had no family responsibilities, and he fought solely to keep up his reputation for toughness, sometimes without even wanting to fight. And lately, when he decided it was time to revive his reputation, he would retire to the little room at the back of the store, swallow great swigs of liquor, and come out primed, ready to explode at the first word said to him. No one was spared; the idea was to have a good, noisy brawl that would be heard and talked about.

Geminiano was a cheerful Negro, tame on the outside but a bit prickly inside. Whenever anyone said something that offended him, he would stop in mid-smile and become solemn. The kids liked him because he gave them rides in his wagon and sometimes handed out scrapings of sugar, so clear and smooth it was almost a shame to break them up for eating; their parents respected him for his insistence on dotting every "i" and crossing every "t" in his business

14

arrangements. For him a deal was like a vow made to a saint; it had to be made good, come hell or high water. He permitted himself no "wish I had's," useless efforts to get himself out of an agreement that had become unprofitable. Even Geminiano's wife complained at times, saying that he was missing the boat by being so scrupulous when others were not. He would explain:

"I'm black, so my slate has to be very clean. I can't afford to be lax. If I let people scribble on it, there's no telling what would happen."

As might be expected, Amancio Mendes' blustering remarks eventually reached Geminiano's ears. When he heard, Geminiano spent the rest of the day and nearly all night thinking about the best way to keep his slate clean. He and Amancio got along fairly well, but without any backslapping. There was a coolness between them, on Amancio's part because of a certain prejudice against dark skin, and on Geminiano's because he disapproved of Amancio's hotheaded behavior. Aware that an argument could have serious consequences, they saw each other only on those occasions that were strictly necessary in a small town. And now Amancio had come out with a rattle-brained insult— behind Geminiano's back, too. Geminiano had a problem.

Why this uncalled-for provocation? Could Amancio be in league with the strangers? If he was, he must be expecting some reaction . . . Well, there was going to be no reaction as long as Amancio didn't insult him to his face.

Geminiano had an old pistol in a drawer at home; he would shift it to his belt and, for the rest of it, behave as

15

if nothing had happened. He would even go on trading at Amancio's store, no matter how much effort it took to speak naturally. If they had to fight, it would be a clean fight—but Amancio would have to start it.

Amancio remained alone in his defense of the strangers; everyone else felt that Geminiano, as owner of the wagon, was the one to decide how it should be used. Because someone has money or brags that he has, can he rub your nose in it and take over what belongs to you? If that sort of thing were allowed, tomorrow one of them might be sitting quietly at home, maybe lying in his hammock, when a stranger walks in and without even a "Good morning" for starters, says "I like your house, I'll take it, here's the cash, better start getting your things out, or just leave them there and I'll pay someone to throw them out."

Geminiano was right, obviously, and he could count on all of them if the men came for revenge. No one should pay any attention to Amancio; he was well known for antagonizing everyone in the hope of starting a fight. Had they all been against Geminiano, it was a sure thing that Amancio would have been for him. Who could understand someone like that? No wonder Amancio lived all alone, estranged from family and friends. The few who still bothered with him and looked for him in the little gullies near the river or the hayfields around the town, where he usually dropped after a drinking bout, did it more out of pity than friendship. Friendship is a two-way street, but with Amancio Mendes there was no return lane; whoever gave him a helping hand ran the risk of having it bitten.

What saved Amancio was his big heart, but it only showed after some personal upset, while he could still remember it. On those occasions he was almost unrecognizable: nothing was too good for his customers; he gave presents right and left, insisted they buy on the cuff, canceled all debts, and got angry with those who refused his bounty—he was almost disgusting in his efforts to please! But it did make it awkward to start a fight with Amancio . . .

When Dr. Nelorio (who arrived at Manirema with two deaths to his credit—family feud—and took elaborate care never to show his temper) was shouted out of the store because he wanted an adjustment on a sack of worm-eaten beans, he did not protest or stop speaking to Amancio. He merely remarked later that Amancio Mendes was a cross Manirema had to bear. But for Geminiano it was quite different. He had neither the social position nor the objectivity of Dr. Nelorio, who had no need to show who he was to be respected and could afford to let certain things pass without losing face. Geminiano's reputation cost a little more. That was why everyone dreaded the outcome of Amancio's insult.

Father Prudente sent for Geminiano on the pretext of needing him to haul some tiles; he hemmed and hawed a bit before finally pouncing on his subject.

"I heard we came close to losing your wagon."

Geminiano did not catch on at first; then, like corn on the cob, his teeth showed in a grin, and he explained:

"No sweat. I just told him the way we do things around here."

"So there was no argument?"

"I didn't give him time. When I got annoyed, I whipped the donkey and left."

"Well done, Geminiano. When one is unwilling, two don't fight."

Father Prudente thought a while, whistling between his teeth. When he knew what he wanted to say he began by repeating himself.

"You did the right thing. You kept up your standards and avoided a fight."

Geminiano understood from this that he had the priest's backing. He said:

"Some people don't think so."

"Well, so what? He's only one fish in the pond."

"I know, Father. But I got very upset. I still am."

Father Prudente went back to his whistling. He dared not speak without thinking, or attempt to discharge his obligation with some trite moralizing. Eventually he spoke:

"It has to be one of two things, Seu Geminiano. Either he said it to show off, or he said it to offend you. If it was just careless talk, no offense can be taken. But if he did it on purpose, he must be dying for you to retaliate. If you retaliate, you are doing exactly what he wants you to do. If he can't live without fighting, let him go and punch rocks, bang his head against the wall. A man like you should fight only to defend his home, or his family, or his life. Of course, if he ever lays a finger on you, you would have every right to strike back."

Geminiano looked into the distance, thinking. Father Prudente whistled his low little whistle, discreet and respectful.

"And if he keeps on talking?" Geminiano said.

"Well, what's the matter with that?"

"I'll end up losing face if I don't get even."

"No you won't. No man can make another lose face. When one man's talk demoralizes another, it is because he is already demoralized. What counts is not what one man says but what everybody can see. You disguise yourself as a stranger and go from door to door asking what kind of a person is Geminiano Dias, and then you tell me what they said."

Geminiano laughed, feeling thwarted but happy. Father Prudente sure knew how to handle words. Each man's talk should be measured out to him in yards on the day of his birth. That way anyone talking to hear himself talk would be using up his yardage—one fine day he would open his mouth and nothing would come out but air.

Suddenly Geminiano remembered the pistol under his shirt—big and heavy as an ax, useless and uncomfortable. Father Prudente noticed his embarrassment and smiled. He was not going to say anything, but neither would he pretend to be unaware of it. Geminiano must not be spared the shame; it was part of the lesson. At last he relented:

"When do you think you can bring my tiles?"

"Next week, sir, if you are not in a hurry."

19

THE DECISION not to show interest in the strangers until approached by them seemed to have been reached too quickly, without taking everybody's natural curiosity into account. When the strangers first appeared, the more independent people began to hang around near the fence of the campsite in the hope of establishing contact, but they got nowhere. They stayed there hour after hour, putting up with the heat and flies, staring at the camp. The men inside, whether working or taking it easy, seemed quite indifferent to them. As the townspeople had nothing to report on their return, they invented exchanges with the strangers, and others then felt the urge to have a look. Many of them took snacks—candies, cookies, leaf-wrapped packets of manioc flour—and ate carelessly, their minds on the camp, spilling crumbs everywhere, attracting ants, stamping on them, slapping at their legs.

Without appearing to notice their inquisitive neighbors, the strangers apparently were annoyed by the scrutiny and began hanging out clothes on a rope stretched along the fence where the crowd was. Some of the more persistent tried to stand on the barbed wire, but the staples shot out of the fence posts from the weight and the wire fell before they had a chance to see a thing. As there was nothing to be gained staring at a screen of clothing (it looked as if the men would never take it down), the townspeople resigned themselves to watching from afar. A man going by on a horse could catch a glimpse of life on the other side of the fence by standing up in the saddle—

scenes of work, play, rest, isolated scenes that had no meaning for anyone unable to see the whole, the design that ordered it.

At night the campfires and the lanterns burned late; the townspeople could see the glare through the trees. And when the wind was right it carried voices and laughter and even shreds of music, but no one paid attention any more. It had all become a part of the natural night scene, and did not disturb the peace.

Manirema was no longer interested in the men. If anyone spoke of them at all, it was as if mentioning an everyday occurrence—the heat, sickness, high prices. Even Amancio Mendes, once so ready to shout in their defense, now appeared not to care. In effect it was as though Julio Barbosa's property were still abandoned—or as if those men had always lived there; so much so, in fact, that when Geminiano announced he was carting sand for the camp (he did not say it for news value, he was merely giving a reason for being unable to take on a job immediately) no one raised an eyebrow, none thought it strange, none doubted him. Transporting firewood, foodstuffs, construction materials, anything that fit inside the cart, even loose pigs, was Geminiano's trade. The wagon was almost a public utility; it served anyone with enough patience to wait his turn. When the hauling of a particularly heavy load obliged Geminiano to stop for a few days for repairs, everyone took an interest, wanting to know the extent of the damage, how long it would take to fix, whether Geminiano had the necessary ready cash (this was cunning because if Geminiano had to borrow money or accept an advance, the lender considered himself morally justified in asking for priority). Crowds came to see the wagon and volunteer their opinions on the best way to mend it. The broken-down cart was like a sick relative.

Now Geminiano was working for the strangers. They must have waited their turn; Geminiano favored no one, and certainly not those men. But why was it taking so long? His customers began to get impatient.

"What's all this sand you're carrying, Gemi? When are you going to finish?"

"They're the ones who know. They waited their turn."

"How much longer?"

"I have no idea."

It was a month since he had started on the job, making one, two, three trips a day, according to how it went; and he still did not know when he would be through. On the washerwomen's beach there was already a huge hole, by which it could be imagined how much sand was piling up inside the encampment.

"Why do they need so much sand?"

"They're building. What else could it be? They're doing a lot of building."

Curiosity came back in a flash. They had to know what kind of building and what for, and only Geminiano could tell them. Every time he crossed the bridge a crowd surrounded him, more people tagging along every place he went; when he reached the square he was dragging a whole mob, or they were dragging him. No sooner had he answered one question than another was shouted at him; the pushy types jumped onto the wagon and tugged at Geminiano's clothes, insisting on his attention; some even took him by the chin, others ran alongside pulling at his sleeve or trouser cuff, leaping up goat-like to hear what he had to say. Every once in a while someone got careless and had his foot run over by the wheel and went hopping off on the other foot, giving up but watching the excitement until it disappeared in the distance.

From this confusion of many questions and very few answers, it was deduced that the men were making repairs, lean-tos, improvements of all kinds, but exactly what no one could tell. Geminiano would only say that they were knocking down walls, putting up walls, roofing, plastering, painting.

"So they're going to stay there forever?"

"I doubt it."

"And what do they live on? What do they eat?"

"There's no shortage of food. Every night supplies come from somewhere."

If that's how it was, they would not be coming to the town. Why would they come, if they had everything they needed in the camp? Gone were the dreams of revenge when the strangers would come meekly asking for supplies.

One evening at the store, quite unexpectedly—the subject of discussion was still the shortage of salt bacon—Amancio shocked everyone by saying that the following day he was going to pay a visit to the campsite.

"You're going to do what?"

"I'm going to see what those guys are up to."

"Did they send for you or something?"

"Send for me? D'you think I'm a dog? I'm going on my own. I've made up my mind and I'm going."

"Well now, you be careful, Amancio."

"What of? They don't have fur, and I'm no burr."

It was not a bad idea, having someone go over there with an open mind to look around, socialize, talk things over. Why hadn't they thought of it before? After all, the men were on Manirema land and subject to the regulations of the town; they would have to explain what they were doing there.

But if Amancio went, the whole thing might backfire. The right man for the job was Dr. Nelorio. He could go there, talk, and come back informed; no one would have the nerve to talk back to him, and if they did they would be sorry. Another one who might be entrusted with such a mission was Marianito from the notary's office, who had an extraordinary knack for poking his nose into other people's business, always smiling and pulling them by the arm to whisper in their ears as if everything were a deep, dark secret—a trick he had learned in the seminary. Amancio was the least likely person to go, being prickly as a porcupine, ready and willing to take offense at the slightest provocation. As he was not clever with words, he would get so badly tangled in his own tongue that the only way out would be to fight. He was the type to get into a brawl in order to stop it and then end up fighting with the brawlers.

"Maybe more than one person should go?"

The speaker was Manuel Florencio, a carpenter; a moderate man, practiced in the arts of filing and sanding. But Amancio's answer was short and cutting.

"I don't see why. I've done without a tail till now."

Manuel Florencio shrank inside and out. He had no luck with Amancio, never got anything from him but rebuffs. But when Amancio woke up in a gutter, bruised and muddied after a night of booze and carousing, the one who picked him up was usually Manuel Florencio, swearing each time that it would be the last.

"What if they don't like the idea?" asked Justino Moreira.

The question remained unanswered. Amancio was measuring out a foot of rope tobacco for a farmer. He marked it, cut the tobacco two fingers in front of the mark (in the customer's favor), and put the measuring stick away.

"Anything else, boss?"

The customer asked for a few more small items—gunpowder, lead, caps; he accepted some roach killer as a bonus, paid, and left the store. Amancio ended the matter.

"If they don't like it, let them take a dose of bicarbonate. While I'm there they'll have to swallow what I have to say."

Now it was better for the others not to insist. The more they tried to change his mind, the more mulish he would get. The only hope was that he would change his own mind, or forget all about it in his sleep, as had happened before. Anyway, nobody there was Amancio's keeper.

Early next day, dressed all in white, with a white hat

25

turning yellowish and ankle boots of raw leather, Amancio dropped in at Manuel Florencio's house on the square. He wanted Manuel to check on the store every once in a while, and said he would not be away long. Observing Amancio closely and noticing no sign of a gun under his clothing, Manuel breathed easier. The outcome would depend on the strangers and how they treated Amancio.

"You had coffee? Have some before you go. It's good and hot!"

"I don't need any. I ate a hunk of cheese and some other stuff. I'm getting a move on while it's still cool."

Manuel Florencio had intended to finish some door panels but could not get started. That notion of Amancio's just wasn't fitting. What if the men did not like it and threw him out; who could rest easy in the town after that? Sleeping dogs should be left to lie. Unless Amancio was just pretending. If he came back saying he had marched right into the compound, bargained and belched, fought with and shaken them, it would be best not to show disbelief, or he would be obliged to go and make fact of his fiction. Bravado faked once cannot be faked again.

Manuel Florencio walked to the door and glanced out at the notary's place on the high side of the square. Knots of people were at the windows or standing outside, staring and pointing. From there one could see the road beyond the bridge, the pasture lands, and the campsite, half hidden by trees. Manuel dropped everything and walked across the square, reaching the notary's just as Amancio rounded the corner of the camp fence.

26

"He's really going. He's the kind who would milk a wild-cat."

"And he's going in the front way, the old devil."

"It's now or never. If he comes right out it's because he was thrown out."

Amancio's white hat disappeared behind the high grasses at the edge of the fence, reappeared for a moment farther on, and disappeared again.

"Didn't I tell you he'd go? That Amancio is a man!"

Now anything might happen. Some voiced the thought that there would be nothing to it, the men would receive Amancio at the gate, chat about nothing, and send him about his business; he would come back saying he had been there and talked to them (he would not be telling a lie), and whatever else he told them would be invented on his way back to town. But others said that Amancio was not the type to be sent away at the door, especially when he was dressed up like that. To soothe the worries, Manuel Florencio reported that he had been with Amancio before he set out and that he had noticed no bulge of a weapon.

"It doesn't make any difference—he can always come back and get his carbine. I saw him cleaning it yesterday."

Hearing this, Manuel mentally resolved to hide the carbine before Amancio returned.

About that time Geminiano came into sight with the day's first cartload of sand. The crowd took off toward him in a rush, leaping over holes in the road and the pile of tin shavings discarded by the tinsmith, João José.

"He went! Amancio went! He's there!" they shouted, all out of breath.

"Where?" asked Geminiano, a bit taken aback by the uproar.

"He went to talk to the men. He's already there."

"Talk? He won't be able to. No one there has time."

"He's there right now, talking."

"I'll believe it when I see it."

"Right. Go see if you can find out what's going on."

Geminiano did not reply; instead, he made a sort of hissing noise with his lips. The mob interpreted it as disdain for the assignment, but Serrote took it for marching orders.

Watching the wagon rumble away, iron-bound wheels biting into the ground, sand piled high, shovel thrust in ready for the unloading, a lot of them envied the driver the swaying contraption which would soon be entering the mysterious territory.

Manuel Florencio returned to his shop, fiddled with his board, but could not get going. He remembered Amancio's request and grabbed at the excuse. How could he possibly work and watch the store at the same time?

The door to the store had been left open a crack; it widened and narrowed with the breeze, making the hinges creak and groan. Manuel pushed it open, blinking to get his eyes used to the gloom, and scraped his head on a stalk of bananas hanging from a beam. A rat squealed and vanished into a pile of garden spades. If Amancio didn't get off his butt and set some traps, he was going to have to ask the rats' permission to use the store. Never had Manuel seen a place so slovenly. Sleeping right there in the back between bags and crates of provisions, how on earth could Amancio let the rats run around as if they owned the place?

Manuel Florencio propped the door ajar with a hatchet and opened all the windows. The fresh air rushed in, setting asway the hanging buckets and coffee pots, the strings of onions, reins, and horsehair ropes, even a couple of harnesses. The floor needed a sweeping, the counter a wipe with a damp cloth to get rid of tell-tale circles from the glasses of *cachaça*,* scattered grains of sugar, salty grease from the sides of dried beef, stickiness from raw sugar cake, spilled flour. Manuel found a broom and water, sprinkled the floor so that the dust would not rise, and set about his cleaning.

The customers began to arrive in dribs and drabs. A small boy wanted raw sugar for making citron jam; only the very clear type would do, his mother had told him. Manuel let the boy choose his own and went on sweeping, bending occasionally to pick up a coconut, a roll of tobacco, or a pair of slippers that had fallen from the pile. A little old black lady, all shrunken and shaking in speech and self, wanted six inches of chewing tobacco, and would Seu Amancio have the kindness to give her good measure. Manuel dropped his broom, twisted and broke off a generous hand's-breadth of tobacco, and gave it to the old lady. She sniffed it, bit off a piece to see if it was any

* A sugar-cane liquor, the local "white lightning."

good, and began to untie her handkerchief. Manuel held her tiny fist, old, frail and gray.

"No need, grandmother. It's free."

Trembling, she quickly gathered up tobacco, handkerchief, and money.

"May the Good Lord repay you, Seu Amancio. May He pay you well." And she turned and left, shoving tobacco and hankie into her skirt pocket.

Others came in, mostly men wanting to pass the time of day.

"Ho, Seu Manuel. So you're shopkeeper now?"

Manuel explained and asked if there was any news of Amancio. No one knew anything definite, but they felt optimistic; the delay was a good sign, a sign of lingering talk—much tattle, no battle.

More straggled in to sit on the filled burlap bags (respecting the flour and avoiding the salt), and even on the rolls of barbed wire, legs outstretched to avoid the barbs; some dipped handfuls of peanuts from a sack, ate them, and put the shells in their pockets to hide the evidence; some nibbled at the manioc flour or chewed corn, beans —whatever was closest—and blew out the chaff onto the floor.

His cleaning done, Manuel sat on the edge of the counter, half on and half off. The conversation warmed up.

"Amancio did the right thing. To find out if there's a wildcat in the forest you have to get close. If you keep your distance you'll never know if it's a wildcat or just a tame fawn, the kind that eats out of your hand. Except for Geminiano, and he's close-mouthed lately, who else has seen those men close enough to say whether they're wildcats or fawns?"

It was Dildelio Amorim, speaking like the hunter he was.

"It's those buildings I don't understand. Geminiano surprises me: he goes there, sees everything, and says nothing."

"I don't think Geminiano knows anything. He's just a jobber. They're not likely to tell him much."

"Well, if they've got anything to hide, they're not going to open up with Amancio either."

"Amancio's different. He doesn't work for them and he doesn't depend on them. He can look at things more objectively."

"I think we've all been making a mountain out of a molehill. The men are peaceful—they don't bother anyone."

"They don't bother anyone *now*. No one knows yet what they're up to. It's all very mysterious."

By now the store was crowded and people were even standing outside leaning in the windows trying to hear the talk inside. Occasionally someone at the edge of the crowd ventured an opinion that never reached the ears of the insiders but was loudly debated or upheld by the outsiders. Conversation was getting extremely difficult.

When somebody said that there was news at the notary's, they emptied out of the store like beans from a

31

bushel, everyone in a rush to get there first, the older ones puffing along behind, grumbling about the others' hurry, as if the supply of news would disappear because of the demand.

What was being said at the notary's was not really earth-shaking. A boy on a pack mule had ridden past the camp and saw men playing *peteca** behind the fence. He stopped awhile to watch; grown men playing *peteca* are not seen every day. One of the men was all in white, even his hat—sort of peculiar, playing *peteca* in a hat; the brim must make it hard to see. The men argued more than they played and once one of them got angry and stomped off. The game went on with those who were left, and so did the arguments. The worst complainer was the man in white, he seemed to be the owner of the *peteca*.

The crowd considered the information from every angle but could not make head nor tail of it.

"Amancio playing *peteca*? It doesn't make sense."

"The kid probably invented the whole thing."

"Where'd he go, anyway? We'd better talk to him."

Nobody knew who or where the boy was. He had passed by riding pillion on a pack mule, crossed the square, and vanished.

"Where does he live? Whose kid is he?"

A boy leading a pack train might live anywhere; he is

---

* A form of shuttlecock, made of a leather pouch holding brightly colored feathers and flattened at the base. The game of the same name is played by batting the *peteca* with the palm of the hand, always keeping it aloft.

always far from home, he might have no parents at all; he is just a boy leading a pack train, selling firewood, watermelons, cassava, what-have-you. Now he's here, now he's gone. Who could find him in a world full of boys?

But Amancio playing *peteca* with strangers . . . What a crazy notion. If he was fooling around like that he must be aiming at something else. And what kind of men were they, wasting their time on a silly game when, according to Geminiano, there was so much work to do? The story just did not sound right; something was missing, it needed explaining.

When Geminiano's wagon was seen on the road, the whole crowd took off in a rush once more, mindless of the distance. More people poured out of the houses, many of them running because they saw others running, not knowing where they were going or why they were running. Frightened women came to the windows crossing themselves—so many men running in the streets could only mean disaster or evil-doing. Whenever they saw a friend they called out for an explanation, but no answers came, or they came in summary gestures. Nobody stopped, nobody wanted to miss anything.

Once the wide bridge road was reached, the mob fanned out and slowed down, as there was no need to run so hard —Geminiano was coming closer and that was the only road; also, many of them were beginning to feel uncomfortable pain under their ribs.

Geminiano was not pleased to see the crowd. So many people only made things more difficult, they would scare

33

Serrote and hold him back, and he still had two trips to go. He slapped Serrote's back with the reins and pretended there was nobody in his way. The crowd opened up to let him pass, but the wagon had barely reached the clearing in the middle when Geminiano saw he had fallen into a trap.

"Make way! Make way! Look out for the donkey!" he shouted, shaking the reins and not moving at all.

Unable to proceed, old Serrote lifted his head, swelled out his chest muscles, and pawed at the ground in an effort to show his master he understood the orders coming over the reins.

People yelled, pushed, pulled; Geminiano could not understand what all the shouting was about, so he shouted too.

"Make way! Make way! Watch out for the wheels! Look out for your feet! Careful of the donkey! Move!"

It was no use. The crowd would not move. Serrote was being held by the brake, by the neck, by the ears; there were even people pressing down on the wheels to hold them still. Geminiano sighed and gave up.

"What happened to Amancio?"

"Did he get in?"

"What did the men do?"

"Are they really playing *peteca?*"

"Was there a fight?"

With some difficulty Geminiano was able to tell them that he had not seen Amancio, that he knew nothing of either *peteca* or a fight; it was all very quiet in the camp, everyone at work.

34

"At work, my eye! They were playing *peteca* with Amancio."

"I didn't see it."

"A boy saw them."

"He did? Then they were."

"Have they finished?"

Geminiano got angry and exploded:

"Do you want to know something? I've got work to do! Pardon me. Come on, Serrote!" and he whipped the donkey, forcing his way through the disappointed mob.

Some of them could not get out of the way in time and had their feet chewed by the cart wheels, others got their ribs bruised, one was bumped in the chest by Serrote's head and went off coughing and swearing revenge—a shot between the eyes, a whack on the kidneys. The wagon rolled away, rattling its bolts, Geminiano urging the donkey on to make up for lost time.

THE SUN was already high when Amancio returned. The others were eating but Manuel Florencio was still minding the store, waiting, killing time by tidying things up. Amancio came in, saw the clean-swept floor, the wiped-off counter, the aggressive orderliness of it all.

"*Compadre,** you've got possibilities. Want to be my partner?"

---

* Literally, co-father. A father and a godfather are *compadres;* a mother and a godmother are *comadres*. Godparents are also *compadre* and *comadre* to each other.

Manuel smiled but had no intention of letting Amancio digress.

"How was it?" he asked, pretending to rearrange some bottles on a shelf.

Amancio broke open a peanut shell, tossed the nuts into his mouth, and replied as he chewed.

"I went and I came back."

"So I see. But what happened in between?"

Amancio did not answer at once. He went around back of the counter, ran his eye over the bottles to find the one in use, found it, and looked for a glass.

"They didn't bite me. We talked, we fooled around. They're open types, nothing to hide."

"You played *peteca*."

"*Peteca?* Who said?"

"We heard."

Amancio smiled, his eyes distant, then changed the subject.

"He who knows, knows; if he doesn't know, let him find out, my Uncle Lindolfo used to say. He was a priest, did I ever tell you about him? A sober, reliable man. My mother's brother. One day he took off his cassock, tossed away his rosary, and went off to become a revolutionary. My mother nearly died. They say he killed dozens of men. Then he was amnestied. I think he's still living, teaching Latin, but I don't know where. I once had a picture of him that was in the papers. Dressed like an officer, he was, with two revolvers in his belt. By the size of the cases they must have been forty-five. I need one of those. Yes sir, my

Uncle Lindolfo, Father Lindolfo, with guns in his belt . . . If my mother had seen it she wouldn't have believed it. But even in his uniform he was the spitting image of my mother. He always looked more like a woman, or so they said at home."

While he was talking, Amancio drained two quick glasses. Now he kept glancing from bottle to glass and vice versa, wanting to go on and not wanting to. Manuel Florencio was in no hurry. He knew Amancio well—it was no use pressing him. Amancio was a cunning sort of donkey, the kind that balks just to see how upset his owner can get.

Amancio knocked off one more drink, sneakily, as if he were not the owner of all the liquor in the shop; he rolled the taste around his tongue, taking his time about it.

"They've got good liquor over there. Still in the barrel. I'm going to get some when they bottle it. They say it's not ready yet. To me it's as good as it will ever be. It must be an excuse for not handing it out. But I'm going to get my bottles, I don't care what they say."

Manuel listened patiently, his mind on what was still to come. Amancio filled and swallowed another glassful, quickly, without warning. Opening the drawer to look for cigarettes, he came upon the money from Manuel's sales.

"Hey! When I go out things improve," he said as he raked up the cash, counting out loud. He picked out a bill and handed it to Manuel. "Your salary, *compadre*."

Manuel twisted away in protest.

"Don't be silly. I don't want it, Amancio."

37

Thwarted by the refusal, Amancio offered:

"Well, then, take something you need. I insist."

"I don't want anything. Lord's sakes—"

Amancio looked around, irritated; he was losing the argument and he could not stand it. He grabbed for a rope of smoked sausage and tossed it at Manuel. He knew Manuel liked smoked sausage.

Manuel accepted it, giving in. After all, smoked sausage rounds out a meal nicely, if it isn't too salty. He rolled up his present, wrapped it in an old newspaper, and wiped his hands on a sack of flour.

"Well, thanks, Amancio. But you still haven't said anything about the men," he complained, in a last try before he had to leave.

"*Compadre,* I've got news for you. Every one of us has been barking up the wrong tree."

Manuel waited for clarification, but it looked as if Amancio was in no mood to explain.

"In what way?" he pressed.

"If all of us here were like them, Manirema would be a little corner of heaven, or some foreign nation."

This enthusiastic approbation did not clear things up much.

"But what do they want? What kind of tune are they playing?"

"They don't want anything. They're not playing any tune."

"What about the buildings they're putting up?"

"Exaggeration. It's all bitty stuff. A lean-to. A pigsty. Repairs. Don't listen to all that nonsense."

Whether Amancio was holding out or just waiting to be coaxed into talking, Manuel was not going to insist any longer. He could keep his little secrets.

"Well, you take over the store now because I've got work to do," Manuel said, leaving abruptly and forgetting his package. Amancio did not notice it immediately, but when he did he picked it up and was about to heave it into the alley. He stopped himself in time, though, and left it on the counter to give to the first beggar that came by. Even in this Manuel was coming out on top: when had Amancio been known to give a rope of smoked sausage to a beggar?

For Amancio, Manuel Florencio was an itch. Him and his mania for honesty, for making the world aware of its sins, by saying things nobody likes to hear. Who did he think he was? God's private secretary? Record keeper of the world? Whoever he thought he was, Amancio had to admit that he thought and acted right. Manuel never got into arguments, never got excited, held no grudges; when he had to, he showed his displeasure right then and there and the slate was wiped clean. That was why a lot of people disliked him. But only one person had to criticize him for Amancio to rush to his defense. Who in Manirema was better than Manuel Florencio? If he stepped on a tail now and then, it was because there were too many tails lying around to step on, the fault was with the be-tailed. And he knew how to be a friend, unfailing in time of need. If it were not for Manuel's friendship, Amancio would surely have been dead by now, in a fight or an accident. And what did Manuel get in return? Kicks and curses. Why should he waste his time helping Amancio?

39

For credits? What was the advantage of being a creditor if debts were not collected? Mulling it over, Amancio discovered that he really detested Manuel when he was there, but was forced to like him when he was not.

After lunch the store filled up again. Each one came on the pretext of purchasing something, bought it (or didn't), and stayed on to pass the time of day. Amancio knew perfectly well what they wanted, but pretended not to catch on.

"What's the matter with everyone today? It almost looks like this is the only store in town," he snarled at those customers not deserving much consideration, the kind that came to him only when they could not get what they needed elsewhere, or wanted to find something out.

Waiting on them all, weighing cured beef, measuring flour, climbing the ladder to bring down a bundle of house slippers for a customer to choose from, reaching under the counter for a package of nails, wrapping up a tiny roll of stick cinnamon, measuring and cutting rope tobacco, taking in cash and giving change, Amancio remained close-mouthed. But people who had been waited on did not leave and new customers kept coming in, pushing and shoving; if anyone happened to drop a bill, a penknife, or anything at all, there was hardly enough room to bend over and pick it up. Cakes of soap, boxes of rifle caps, bundles of candles, bags of milled salt, all were passed over the heads of the audience, as it were, to those unable to reach the counter, amid great fussing and squeezing and complaining.

Amancio eventually tired of all the noise. He folded his arms and bellowed from the back of the store:

"That's all, folks. I've already sold enough for a whole month. Now get out because I'm going to close."

"Oh, no! You can't do that! My cartridges! Twenty-four caliber!"

"My crackers! They're for a sick man!"

"Don't close, Amancio!"

"I've closed. I'm not going to sell everything out in one day. Come on, let's go. Let's go! Out, everybody!" And he began to push his customers out with the end of his measuring stick, using it as if it were a cattle goad. "Get going. No one's staying."

Some tried to hang onto the edge of a crate or the ears of a burlap bag, but they got a sharp rap across the knuckles and had to let go. In less than no time the store was emptied, every window shut and locked, the door barred from the inside. Out in the street they were still reluctant to go, forming a swarm by the door and all talking at once, trying to find someone to blame for the store-keeper's behavior, protesting his lack of consideration, swearing never to set foot inside his rotten little shop again, calling down horrendous curses on his head—but always hoping that Amancio would change his mind and open up again. They pressed their faces to door and windows, trying to find a crack to peek through. Nobody could see a thing but anyone able to get his eye to a crack was promptly dislodged by someone else who wanted to look.

The uproar continued until Amancio decided to put an

41

end to it once and for all by opening the window a slit and firing a shotgun over the heads of the mob. The double charge echoed loudly in the narrowness of the alley, frightening birds and chickens in neighboring yards, and reverberating in the woods at the edge of the river.

The crowd disappeared with the smoke, and when Amancio opened the window to investigate the effect, with the exception of a few hats scattered about on the ground, there was no sign that anybody had been in the alley.

IN THE MIDDLE of the afternoon, when the sun was lengthening the shadows in the square, the wagon turned the corner and entered the alley. It was covered with a makeshift awning, a piece of canvas held up by a pole and two props, and when it stopped at the door of the store three men got down. They wore belted jackets with buttoned pocket flaps, the sort of thing foreigners often wear, but seldom seen in Manirema. They got down, straightened their clothes as if they were going to have their pictures taken, and knocked on the door.

Nothing happened, and they turned to look inquiringly at Geminiano, who had remained seated on the wagon.

"Might have gone out," he called. "Let me try."

Geminiano jumped to the ground, listened at the keyhole, and then shouted into it.

"Hey, Amancio! It's us!"

It was not long before the door was opened a crack, then dragged wide open.

"Come on in," said Amancio, lowering his shotgun.

Noting the men's surprise, he justified himself: "I had to get a gun because of some jerks out there. Come on in. Come in, Gemi."

Gemi. So that's how it was. Geminiano did not know whether he liked it or not. He excused himself, saying that he still had to water the donkey and get ready for dinner. His wife did not like to wait.

"I'll be going. I got you here, didn't I?"

The men entered in silence. Amancio closed the door.

These visits became a regular thing and people got used to the idea. As soon as the men arrived, the customers began to leave, voluntarily, before Amancio asked them to go. Nobody balked, nobody maneuvered to stay. And, stranger still, nobody tried to find out what was discussed in those long sessions behind the closed door, between the stalks of bananas and strings of onions. It might have been that the townspeople were getting tired of those men and their interminable repairs, the apparent senselessness they no longer tried to decipher. The less said about it the better; more time and gray matter left over for the daily grind.

But then Geminiano started to grumble. At first it was only a vague complaining with no clear aim or motive, and the townspeople were inclined to blame it on fatigue or boredom with the sameness of a job that seemed to have no end. Even Serrote walked between the shafts dispiritedly, his head down in resignation, as if he were looking to the ground for some justification for the utter absurdity of his labors. Geminiano, once so confident and open, never passing up an opportunity to show his white

43

teeth in a grin that told the world how good it felt to be a proprietor, even Geminiano had come to this—a man uneasy in the driver's seat, shoulders hunched, eyes staring fixedly at Serrote's scrawny haunches, paying no attention to the reins or to where he was heading. If he met anyone in the street or on the road, he lifted his hand in a mechanical gesture that did not even come close to the brim of his hat. If anyone greeted him he seemed not to hear, or he heard long after he had been spoken to.

One day, as he was laboring up a little hill at the end of the square, one of the planks of the wagon came loose and a great pile of sand spilled on the ground. Geminiano dismounted with a bound, stared at the spilled sand, the broken plank, and lost his temper; he gave the cart wheel a furious kick, as though he wanted that to break, too. People who saw came running to the scene wanting to know what had happened, if they could help, and found Geminiano leaning on the wheel, sobbing. Everyone was embarrassed. Should they try to console him, as one does a child, or should they leave quietly, out of consideration for the despair of a man once so well balanced?

Geminiano paid no attention to them but went on lamenting:

"What am I doing, my Father, what am I doing? How am I going to get out of this prison? Why didn't I get out while there was still time? What is going to become of me? I can't stand it any longer! I'm at the end of my rope! I know I'll end up doing something terrible."

Someone detached himself from the crowd and put

his hand on Geminiano's back, saying in a friendly tone:

"Take it easy, Gemi. We're here. We'll help you. It's not something to cry about. The plank broke? Sand spilled? We'll fix it. We'll pick it up. Don't carry on like that. Dry your eyes."

Geminiano gazed at him through a veil of tears and for a second did not seem to recognize him or believe what he had just heard. The man stepped back prudently; Geminiano was not himself and anything might happen. But Geminiano let go of the wheel, threw his arms around the man, and poured out his heart, crying openly now.

"You don't know what I've been through, Dildelio. It's too much for one man."

"Don't take it so hard, Gemi. We'll help you. Every evil has a cure," soothed Dildelio, while trying to free himself from the strangling embrace.

"There's no cure for me, Dildelio. My remedy is a bullet through the head or a cup of poison." He clung tighter to his friend, as if that way he could unload some of his suffering.

The others began to lose their embarrassment and came a little closer. None could think of the right words to console him; all they could do was echo Dildelio.

"Don't take it so hard, Gemi. Lord's sake."

"Just tell us what's the matter, we'll do something about it."

"You're with friends."

"Every evil has a cure."

Dildelio held up his hand, asking for silence.

45

"You're tired, Gemi. Spill the sand off here and go on home, lie in your hammock, and get some rest. We'll spread the sand out so that it isn't all piled up. Come on, everybody! Let's unload the sand!"

"No, no! Don't touch it!" Geminiano cried out in alarm. "You mustn't unload it! I've got to deliver it!"

"Take the day off, Gemi. You're all upset. Go on home. We'll go with you."

Geminiano straightened up and took a deep breath. He looked at the houses, the trees, the sky; he might have been reproaching the landscape for its indifference, or calling on it to witness his suffering. He sighed and said calmly, resigned now:

"There's no way out, Dildelio. I'll deliver the sand. I've got to. It's my fate."

With a long-suffering expression on his face, he peered around, found a piece of wood probably fallen from some pack train, pushed the broken plank into place with it, and, using it as a crossbar, braced the plank. Then he reached for the shovel and began to put the spilled sand back into the wagon. When there wasn't enough sand left to fill the shovel he finished the job with his hands, meticulously collecting every last grain, as if a thimbleful would make a difference in the price of a load. And even after he was up on the driver's seat with the reins in his hands ready for departure, he looked back to see if any sand had been left behind. Finally he shook the reins, spoke softly to Serrote, and started off slowly, defeated.

"Poor old Geminiano. That job will be the end of him,"

46

said Dildelio, gazing after the cart and shaking his head.

"Then why doesn't he leave it? Why doesn't he tell those men to go to hell?" asked somebody in the crowd.

"Everybody knows where his own shoe pinches," Dildelio replied. "If he hasn't left it until now, it's because he can't. God knows what he's putting up with. Didn't you notice how he's changed? This Geminiano isn't the old Geminiano we all knew, and it'll get even worse if he doesn't stop."

It was true. The old Geminiano was a far cry from the one who now went by in his cart; everyone agreed and lamented the change. And, not having anything else to do there in the middle of the road, each went his way, home or to work, inwardly accusing Geminiano. If he had gotten into it with two feet, why not use the same two feet for getting out? They must be weighted with lead.

Time passed and nothing new seemed to happen. Geminiano fixed his wagon and went on carting sand, growing more silent and shrunken each day. The men from the compound continued to visit Amancio at the store; they would arrive unexpectedly and make everyone else leave. Sometimes they stayed far into the night, sometimes they left at once, taking poles and fish hooks down to the river. They never brought back any decent fish, and the townspeople began to wonder about these fruitless fishing trips.

The townspeople remained as ignorant of the men's intentions, or their real occupation, as they were on the day of their arrival. If Amancio knew anything, he guarded

47

his secret well; when he was sounded out he would change the subject jokingly if he was in a good mood, and throw the questioner out if he was in a bad one.

Amancio was getting like his friends in the compound.

THE TIME
OF THE DOGS

THE OUTPOURING OF DOGS was the first tangible sign that the strangers were not really the angels that Amancio said they were. Even if it was done in jest, it showed utter lack of consideration for other people's rights.

The townspeople had noticed two or three days before that the dogs from the compound were becoming noisy and excited, as if they were on the eve of a great hunting expedition. At night the uproar was enough to keep the whole town awake. The general impression was that the men were not giving the animals enough to eat. But why? Meanness? Forgetfulness? Or lack of food? Perhaps Geminiano could offer some explanation.

"Dogs? Demons! Four-footed demons, that's what they are . . ." was all they could get out of Geminiano.

"How many are there, Gemi? It sounds like a whole lot."

"A lot? Double that and then some."

"A dozen? Dozen and a half?"

"A dozen and a half, my foot! A dozen and a half die every day."

"What do they die of?"

"They just die. They fall over, jerk for a minute, and die."

"Where did they get so many?"

"How would I know? They get 'em."

"Where from? Who brings 'em?"

"From far away. From Hell. The devil brings them. It can't be anyone else. Those dogs are a curse!"

It was no good talking to Geminiano. Obviously, all that work was affecting his brain. He seemed to prefer talking to himself rather than to anyone else; any day now he would be running around shouting and cursing like old Inacio Medrado. It seemed as if every town had to have some lunatic in the streets to give its people proof of their own sanity; now that Inacio was dead, Geminiano was surely spoiling to take his place. The men had a lot of dogs in the compound; the racket they made left no room to doubt it. But they could not be getting new dogs every day without letup—that was unreasonable.

The dogs came suddenly, taking them all by surprise. The town was engaged in the usual morning routine of coffee drinking, garden sprinkling, floor sweeping, horse harnessing, when the sound of barking was heard in the distance. People ran to windows, fences, and mudbanks to watch the torrent of dogs race toward the bridge, leaping gullies, climbing slopes, detouring around rocks, all in the wildest disorder, barking constantly.

"Lord! The dogs! Dogs! They're coming this way!"

"The dogs got loose!"

"The dogs!"

"Close the doors! Dogs!"

"The children! Get the children!"

"Run, everybody!"

"Shut everything!"

"Get some clubs!"

Doors banged shut, people shouted, children cried, chickens panicked, mothers scolded, smacked, shook, prayed; men ran here and there, searching for shotguns, pistols, billy clubs. Some just lit cigarettes and went to their windows to watch.

Curiosity notwithstanding, no one dared go outside his house. There was nothing out in the street but animals, grazing indifferently, unaware of the danger or perhaps trusting in the power of their hooves. Even the birds sensed something and retired prudently to the higher branches of trees. Unsuspecting butterflies decorated the edges of the creek, and there they died a few moments later, stepped on, chewed, broken like flowers after a windstorm. The stage was set for the dogs, and they invaded it like devils possessed.

The tidal wave of fur, teeth, paws, tails, and howls irrupted all at once, everywhere sniffing, scraping, rearing, watering rocks, mudbanks, walls and tree roots, scratching at doors, whining, standing on hind legs to see into the houses. They were repelled by the residents with blows from switches, sticks, brooms, even slaps with hand or slipper.

Rebuffed at the front, the dogs surged into the gardens, breaking off plants, ruining vegetable patches, knocking down fences, leaping over walls, chasing and killing chickens, stopping now and then to get rid of the feathers stuck

53

to their snouts with their paws or by rubbing their snouts on the ground. The men tried to scare them off with stones; they picked up rocks and then just held them in midair, not knowing which way to throw—there were so many dogs and they came from all directions. Occasionally a shot and a yelp were heard, muffled in the general uproar.

It was impossible to guess how many there were—those who tried to calculate gave up in despair. More and more were pouring in, it began to look like an endless procession. By midmorning the odor of sweaty fur, urine, and trodden dung was so strong that it invaded the houses and forced the townspeople to burn herbs to drive away the stink.

Shut in their homes, fanning away the smoke, unnerved by the barking, people covered their ears and tried to comprehend this reversal of the order of things: the town was being taken over by dogs and human beings were hiding from them in the dark, not knowing what would happen next. Occasionally a dog appeared inside a house, getting in somehow and scaring people out of their wits. It would look first at one person and then another, choose between them, and come closer, tail wagging. The one favored shrank back, sat on his legs and hid his hands, and tried to find voice to shoo the dog away. It came nearer, sniffed, and waited expectantly; when it was not petted it backed off, disappointed, head down, tail between its legs. Other dogs came in at one door, swept through the house, and searched for a way out through another door, scratching it with their paws, poking at it with their noses, and whining until someone found the courage to go and open it, and then they dashed outside after some invisible prey. There were even instances of dogs entering a house, going directly to the bedroom, and coming out with house slippers, shoes, clothing, anything they could pick up with their teeth; sheets were dragged into backyards, torn to ribbons on rose bushes and *mandacaru* thorns, muddied in gutters, and finally dropped somewhere when they were no longer any good for anything.

Some of them seemed to go into houses merely to unload their bladders; they came, sniffed, chose a place, as often as not a pair of ankle boots put aside in a corner, and quite calmly relieved themselves. Or they circled round and round in the middle of the parlor, back humped and hind legs spread apart, and squeezed out a couple of cigar shapes or a small roll, then wiped their paws two or three times, and went out without looking at anyone, leaving the owners to do the cleaning up. They were insolent and the townspeople put up with it, consoling themselves with the thought that no evil lasts forever.

When they realized that the dogs were in no hurry to leave, people's attitudes began to change. Billy clubs, straps, and shotguns were slowly put away and in their place came fondlings, gentle words, and offers of food. People crowded at windows to whistle for the dogs, snap their fingers, reach out to pet them—fearfully, it is true, but genuinely wanting to be rewarded with a wagging tail. Many went to their kitchens to find food to throw at the dogs' feet. Suddenly it appeared that everybody was crazy about dogs, the more the merrier, and had no aim in life other than to make them happy. If a child picked up the whip readied earlier by his parents and threatened one of the dogs, he was stopped immediately and himself punished with the whip. Respect for the dogs' rights was the order of the day. It was a difficult time for the innocent, the ingenuous, those with good memories.

When it became clear that the animals were not interested in biting anyone (the most they did was growl and show their teeth at anyone who inadvertently annoyed them), but only in giving rein to energies suppressed by the discipline of the camp, the townspeople regained the courage to leave their houses unarmed, and were even amused by the antics of the dogs. Watching them chasing hens in the backyard became a spectator sport. When a hen was lucky enough to escape to the top of a wall or a coffee tree, or into a thicket, hiding and panting and trying to get over its fright, there was always someone ready with a pole to poke at it, and the chase started all over again. Often a hen that was already lame, with balding wings or body feathers missing here and there, was caught and presented to a dog; usually the animal thus honored would merely smell the prize and turn away.

If a dog approached a fountain in the streets, someone always rushed up to cup his hands and spare the animal the inconvenience of drinking from the spout. The Manirema dogs, once lords of those self-same streets, now suffered terrible humiliations. Attacked by the strangers, they were no longer permitted to defend themselves; if they so much as growled, their masters came running to punish them for their impudence. They had to run away or let themselves be bitten if they did not want to be whacked with a stick.

Strange dogs snoozing in doorways were treated with more consideration than children or old folks; people tiptoed to avoid disturbing them, some went as far as to enter their houses through the windows or the back door to keep from stepping on the animals. Many a tender meatball, fried in good fat, was served to them on the best china, the way an honored guest would be treated. The whole town was virtually at the service of the animals; all other activity stopped or was postponed, relegated, forgotten. So long as it was a stranger, any flea-ridden, filthy, mangy dog could find someone to extol in it qualities that none could see but all confirmed. Being a strange dog in Manirema was a very advantageous thing.

But late one afternoon, as if obeying a secret command, all the dogs stopped what they were doing, sniffed the air, wiped their paws, and dashed off in the direction of the camp, tripping up people and each other as they went. They ran out of backyards, trellised enclosures, and rubbish heaps. They were festooned with wood chips, shavings, ashes, twigs, and dried leaves, which dropped from their backs as they ran. The packs coming out of each street spilled into the square, making a flood that flowed in the direction of the bridge, reached the road, and surged toward the compound, leaving behind a mysterious emptiness that the fresh evening breeze soon replaced. On the bridge the squeeze was so terrible that the dogs could be seen climbing over each other or spilling through the railing and falling onto the rocks below, leaving behind the plumb line of a scream.

The townspeople could not decide what to do, afraid of reversing themselves too soon and getting caught without their masks. Unwilling to voice any opinions, they all retired early. In the dark they contemplated the humiliations they had suffered, so easily, almost eagerly, accepted.

Each man was tormented by his private shame. None slept well that night, not even those who had kept out of things, disapproving of the general degradation with a quiet shake of the head; they had discovered that to disapprove in silence was little better than to approve; and they were even denied the cheap consolation of having had the courage to stick together.

The following day the town made a determined effort to return to normal. Nobody wanted even to think of the dogs, but reminders of them were everywhere: in the dung left in passageways of houses, on sidewalks, on the grass in the square, in the stink of urine contaminating every corner, the claw scratches left on doors and walls, the chicken feathers strewn all over the yards and still floating in the air, in the fright not yet faded from children's eyes, and in everyone's embarrassment.

Apparently it was Amancio Mendes who first brought up the subject. The way he spoke gave people the impression that he was sounding them out, trying to provoke them. But no one took the bait, so he smiled and detoured a little.

"I'm thinking of enlarging the store," he announced, sitting on the counter. "I just have to knock out those side walls and add a lean-to. Then I'll carry fabrics, perfumes, better-class stuff."

"Then it'll be a regular shop," commented Dildelio, "like Seu Quinel's."

"Better, maybe. I'm going to hire a good assistant, maybe two."

"What about customers? Seu Quinel's been complaining that nobody buys."

"I'll have plenty of customers. You'll see."

Those present looked at each other out of the corners of their eyes. They understood.

"People say the strangers don't buy anything. They have everything right there—get it from somewhere else."

"People say that, do they? Let 'em talk. While they're talking I'll be selling."

"And when the men go away?" It was Manuel Florencio who spoke, feeling Amancio out for the others.

"Going away, are they? I hadn't heard. Who said so?"

"Nobody. But some day they'll have to go."

"Have to? Well, you wait."

They became a little worried. With the exception of Amancio, who was now a sort of advocate for the men, no one knew very much about the unwelcome neighbors, but whatever they learned was always like this, slightly unpleasant. So they were going to stay. Doing what? Letting dogs loose to terrify people?

"Why did they come snooping around here in the first

place?" inquired Manuel Florencio, not of Amancio or anyone in particular, but in the way a man lets slip a question that has been bothering him for some time. Everyone looked at Amancio, realizing that only he could provide an answer.

Amancio did not care for the question. He replied gravely, reprehensively.

"Snooping? They're not snooping. They came here to work, to bring progress. If folks here don't understand, and hang back, it's because of their backwardness, which really is something! But they're going ahead anyway. If there's anybody who doesn't like it, he can learn to eat less."

No one said anything. They all gazed at the floor, the sacks of dry goods, the merchandise hanging above their heads, the bothersome flies. Amancio seemed to know something, he must know, but he insisted on straying from the subject, making a mystery of it—either for the pure pleasure of irritating them or because the strangers didn't allow him to say anything. But Manuel Florencio, categorical, meticulous, annoying, would not be put off. Twisting a real or imaginary hair in his eyebrow, he began to speak, staring at the floor.

"It's funny. They come to work, to bring progress, to do good. Then why do they stay all burrowed in over there, fenced in, stand-offish, not opening up to anybody, and when they want to have a little fun they let their dogs loose on us?"

"There you go," said Amancio, "you can't understand,

you're head's stuffed with other things. Nobody here understands. Those men are working. I've been there. I saw them."

"You were there playing *peteca*. If that's working . . ."

Amancio muttered, dropped his cigarette, picked it up, dropped it again, stamped on it in a rage, as if it were a poisonous insect, a scorpion or a centipede.

"It was not like that!" he bellowed at last. "You always jump to conclusions. I knew you were going to mess things up. It's all Geminiano's fault. He'll see, that stinking nigger!"

"You're the one jumping to conclusions. Geminiano didn't want to say anything. The person who told us was a boy."

"Whoever it was, it was plain gossip. But it makes no difference. They can talk till their jaws fall off. I'm with the men, and all the rest is bullshit. And if you don't like it, take off your drawers and piss on them."

When he finished Amancio was breathing hard, his teeth clenched. He was so angry he had to scratch several matches before he could light his cigarette. It was difficult to discuss anything with Amancio. Whenever he was wrong, he fell back on threatening, and everyone backed off. Fighting is a lot of work and most of the time it isn't worth the trouble. Amancio himself was the prime example. For all the fights he'd won—most of them—he was never satisfied with the outcome. With anger gone and his head cooled, there was little difference between him and the man he had beaten. In general, winning a

61

fight was no better than losing one. So why fight for nothing?

"Well," said Manuel Florencio, "you say they're working and in the end we will all be better off. Then I believe it, I'll wait and see."

Amancio peered at him, both grateful and suspicious. Manuel at times made him furious, at times heartened him. Manuel was a past master at avoiding a fight without running away. He was past master at a lot of skills a person needs to get along in this difficult world. Manuel the boob. Manuel the fox. Manuel the friend.

"Let's have a little drink, everyone," offered Amancio, turning toward the shelf for bottle and glasses.

The others brightened, mouths beginning to water in anticipation; but Manuel said quietly:

"You all go ahead. Thanks just the same."

"I forgot he was against it. He's practicing up for sainthood," snorted Amancio.

Several people laughed and Amancio was gratified, but Manuel explained:

"It's my stomach. I can't stand the smell of it."

"Hold your nose and toss it back," someone suggested.

"It isn't worth it. I'd rather watch."

"Well, then, eat some peanut brittle. A tapioca cake, anything." It was Amancio, giving an order.

Manuel took a tapioca cake to avoid another argument, while the others were tossing down the liquor, grimacing, snorting, and spitting. If it was so good, he wondered, why was it so hard to swallow?

62

Manuel stayed a bit longer, laughed, chatted, made an excuse, and left. The party would last far into the night, ending eventually in guitar strumming and song, with a few arguments in between, followed by Amancio's gallop through the streets, the wild shots, insults shouted at locked and barred doors, and finally his long sleep in a ditch; Manuel had to be in prime condition for the job of search and rescue.

WHEN HE REACHED HOME, Manuel found Geminiano at the door, sitting in his wagon, waiting. Geminiano hailed him enthusiastically, as he had not done in a long time. He commented that Manuel must be getting rich, or already was, because he did not seem to attach much importance to work these days. Then he jumped down and asked Manuel's leave to come in and talk.

"What's this, Gemi? You look as if you've seen a blue-bird!"

"Me? Yeah. Things have been looking up."

"Ever finish that job?"

"Mo? Finished the first part. Now I'm going to start the second."

"I thought you were tired."

"Me? No! I'm still good for a lot more. But first I need your help. See all those old boards? You're going to change 'em for me."

Manuel resented his bossy manner. Did he get it from dealing with the men in the compound? Well, enough of that.

63

"Ah, I can't, Gemi. I have too much to do. I've got no time to take on repairs."

Geminiano looked at him in fright. He hadn't reckoned with a refusal.

"But you have to. The men are waiting for it."

"Yeah? Well, waiting's good for the health."

"Don't kid around about serious matters, Seu Manuel. The wagon isn't mine any more. It's theirs. They ordered the repairs."

"I'm glad to hear it, Gemi, but I'm not doing any more repairs. Sorry."

Geminiano considered this, stroking Serrote's neck.

"Seu Manuel, I've always had a high regard for you, and it's not going to stop now. Just pretend that the job is still for me and we'll keep it between ourselves."

"But you just said it isn't."

"I said *pretend*. I can tell that you don't think much of the men. You do the job as if it were for me and they don't need to know of our little arrangement."

"No, Gemi. I don't like muddy business. As far as I'm concerned, you don't have to hide anything. You can just tell them that I don't want to do the job."

"Not a chance! They won't like that, Seu Manuel. I can't tell them that. No matter what."

"Then you tell them whatever you like. It was only a suggestion. If it won't do, you think of another. But one thing's sure—I am not going to do the job."

Geminiano looked at him calmly and explained patiently:

64

"You don't seem to understand, Seu Manuel. They sent the wagon for you to mend. I simply can't go back and tell them you won't do the job. That doesn't fit in with their way of doing things."

"Everybody has his own system, Gemi. If what you're saying is their system, then what I said is mine. Now, if you'll excuse me, I'm going in. I've got work to do."

Geminiano was not ready to give up.

"Seu Manuel, think about what you're doing so you won't be sorry later. It's a serious matter. There's no room for whim or fancy. I think you'd better fix the wagon. It isn't much, just a few boards."

Instead of becoming angry, Manuel found Geminiano's insistence rather funny. Oh, what a stubborn man! That was all he needed, to be forced to do a job. And how would they go about forcing him? Someone holding his hand, guiding the sawing and hammering?

"Gemi, it's been good talking to you, but you're getting too insistent. One of these days we'll have another chat, but not about repairs," said Manuel, and he turned to go into his house.

Geminiano rushed to head him off, took him by the arm, and implored:

"Seu Manuel, I'm going to speak frankly. We've never had a disagreement until today. What I'm asking is a favor, for you, not for me. I don't want to see you hurt out of spite." He looked around furtively and added in a low voice, "Those men . . . You don't know what they're like. Don't risk getting on their bad side."

65

Manuel shook his arm free, put his hand on Geminiano's shoulder, and said consolingly:

"Thanks for the advice, but I'll kill my own snakes. See those tools there by the wall? They're bought and paid for—and will be used only on jobs I choose to do. That's my system. Don't misunderstand. You brought up the subject of systems. Wagon repairing I will not do, dead or alive."

Geminiano looked at him with saddened eyes; it might have been pity or it might have been envy. He shook his head slowly and sighed.

"Seu Manuel, when you get into trouble remember that I warned you as a friend. I did what I could, I can't do anything else." He started out, then turned and finished: "I just hope you're as stubborn with them as you are with me. That way they can't blame me for not carrying out orders."

"Don't worry, I can take care of myself," Manuel replied, and went in without another word.

Geminiano climbed slowly onto his wagon, sat down and started thinking. His eyes, fixed on Serrote's thin haunches, were unblinking. Some time later Manuel went to the window to look at the weather, and Geminiano had not moved. Seeing him like that, aimless and still, Manuel thought of the old Geminiano, so sure of himself, full of dignity, considerate of other people's rights. What could have changed that upright man into this useless bundle of dread? Glancing up the street and at the houses across the way, Manuel had the sensation that he was not seeing the old, familiar square, but some other town, remote, inhospitable, evil. Could the old Manirema be ending, disappearing forever? And if so, was it worthwhile continuing to live there? Would it not be better to sell the house, gather up his tools, and take to the roads, going from ranch to ranch and working at whatever was needed?

While Manuel was thinking, Geminiano shook the reins, either on purpose or absentmindedly, and Serrote woke up and began to pull the cart with unwilling steps, like someone serving an endless sentence with no hope of reprieve. Come to think of it, Serrote was not the worst off. He at least knew, or appeared to know; but did the townspeople?

AMANCIO did not drink too much that day, after all; there was no time. In mid-afternoon, on the wagon's return trip, one of the men from the compound got off at the corner of the alley, tugged his clothing straight, and started for the store. The partying inside seemed to disconcert him; he stopped at the door, made a move as if to turn back, then changed his mind. Amancio leapt over the counter and came to greet him.

"An honor, Major! What can I do for you?"

Ignoring this reception, the man came in and looked around, as if to say there were too many people in the store. They understood the look and began to rise, stretching and yawning and scratching their backs, in a naïve attempt to show they were leaving because they wanted to and not because they were being thrown out. The man moved to one side in order not to block the exodus and, when the last one had gone, peered carefully into the back of the store to make sure there was nobody left. Then he went to the door and glanced up and down the alley; he didn't want anyone hanging around. Satisfied with his inspection, he went in and closed the door, as if he were the owner of the store and Amancio only a clerk.

The closed conference did not last long. The people hiding around the corner saw the two leave arguing, Amancio doing most of the talking, talking even when he was putting the key in the lock, the other nodding his head and snapping curt replies. Noticing that they were going to walk up the alley, the spies dispersed in a hurry, none wanting to be caught at the game.

When they reached Manuel Florencio's house, the man from the compound stopped as if to go in, but Amancio barred his way. The man tried to go around him, but Amancio gently but firmly pushed him away. Now their roles were reversed, the stranger doing most of the talking and Amancio nodding his head, leading the man away from the house, the other looking back and nearly digging his heels into the ground to avoid being pushed along. At last it seemed as if Amancio had won, and they continued their walk. At the bridge they parted, Amancio turning back, very preoccupied, passing people he knew without recognizing them, failing to greet them and not returning their greetings, bumping into things, not noticing.

In this state of mind he entered Manuel Florencio's house, puffing and stomping his feet. He stopped in the middle of the workshop, put his hands on his hips, and exploded.

"You and your damn independence!"

Manuel stopped work, eyed him curiously, and waited.

"Why didn't you fix that wagon?"

So that's what it was. But what did it have to do with Amancio?

"I didn't fix it and I won't. We all have reasons for doing what we do," Manuel said evenly, and went back to his planing, uninterested in further conversation.

"We all have reasons, my ass! If you used reason you wouldn't be so obstinate."

Manuel slammed the plane down, raised his head, and said angrily:

"Amancio, you're the boss in your store, I'm the boss in my shop. That is one thing that is going to stay the way it is."

Amancio shook his head in bewilderment, took a turn around the workshop, and came back to the same place.

"You're playing with fire, Manuel. The men are fed up with you. I managed to persuade them to give you until tomorrow. You've got to get that damn wagon fixed by tomorrow even if it takes all night. I'll help you."

Manuel stared at him and let out a roar of laughter, so loud that it frightened off a donkey that had been grazing beside the house.

"Now that's something I'd like to see," he said, still laughing, "somebody forcing me to do a job I don't want to do. There's only one way, Amancio. One bunch of men holding me down and another pushing and pulling my hands on the tools. Can you imagine the results?"

Amancio tried another tactic.

"We've been friends for a long time, Manuel . . ."

"So we have. But what has that got to do with it? Are you by any chance . . ."

"Let me speak. We've been friends for a long time. I came here to ask you a favor. Repair that cart for me."

Manuel picked up the plane; smoothing down the rough edges of a groove, he spoke.

"The more I hear of that wagon, the sicker I get. I don't fix wagons. I didn't ask anyone to cart sand around in a wagon. Let the people who broke it repair it. And what's more, I don't suck up to those people. If you really are a friend, you won't bring up the subject again."

Amancio would not give up. He pressed, threatening now:

"You mean you really won't fix it? Are you willing to pay the price? Because, believe me, there's going to be a backlash from all this. Can I wash my hands of you?"

Manuel went to the window, spat, and walked back.

"You people are certainly peculiar. I work here year in and year out, nobody cares if I'm doing well or badly, if I'm eating or making the sign of the cross over my mouth. Suddenly a broken wagon turns up and the whole world beats a path to my door, insisting that I repair it, plaguing me and hinting about punishment. I am not going to repair anybody's wagon. I am going to make a sign in big letters over there on the wall, 'This Shop Does Not Make Repairs.'

70

That way nobody will be forced to learn Latin to understand me. And I'll put up with any kind of backlash, yessir! What about my rights? A man who's paid is not afraid."

"You're all wrong. You talk as if nothing had changed. Rights? What rights? A man who's paid is not afraid, hah! That's all in the past. Nowadays you don't have to be in debt to be afraid. Why do you think I'm here begging, pleading with you, humbling myself? Do I owe anybody anything? Have you ever seen me afraid? You'd better understand that those times are gone forever."

Amancio stopped speaking and went to the window. He gazed intently at the square, like someone about to leave a place for a long time, with the pain of leaving hurting inside. Now he spoke to the world outside the window, indifferent to the presence of Manuel Florencio.

"Who would have said Manirema could change in so short a time . . . We all used to live in peace, no worries, we went to sleep and woke up and everything was in its rightful place, there was no need to think things out in advance. Today we stop and think before we even say 'Good morning.' What did we do to deserve this? Manuel, we're in a bad way."

Manuel watched him, half pitying, half suspicious. This new side of Amancio—could it be a ruse? Amancio grasped him by the shoulder and said, almost imploringly:

"We've got to stick together, *compadre*. We're going through some very difficult times."

"But why now, Amancio? Or is something else worrying you?"

71

Amancio lowered his head and, hardly audible now, said:

"You know what I'm talking about. I never thought it would come to this, but it has. We've fallen into a trap and I can't see a way out."

"What trap? Aren't you exaggerating?"

"Don't I wish it were a practical joke, the kind we used to play! But I was there. Would to God I hadn't been."

They were silent for a while, absorbing the realities of a situation they had done nothing to create, and which neither of them knew how to remedy.

The silence in the square recalled the peace and quiet of old, but mixed with the recollection came an ominous sense of danger. A large blue butterfly came flying dizzily into the workshop, scraped a wing on the wall, and settled on the handle of an adze. The two gazed at it in wonder, as if they had never seen a butterfly like it, or perhaps astonished that there could still be butterflies in the air. After a while it fluttered around the room a little, and then slipped out into the square as if sucked out by the afternoon breeze, leaving the men even sadder and more uneasy.

Manuel sighed and said with a great effort, forcing the words through his lips:

"I've decided to fix the wagon."

For the first time in his life Amancio threw his arms around his friend, holding him close for a long time. He tried to speak, but his words were too slurred with emotion to be understood.

ON EACH RETURN TRIP Geminiano brought one or two men in his wagon; his passengers got off at the square and stood on a corner or in the shade of the bandstand, showing interest in the passersby, but only in observing them: they spoke to no one, and hesitated to reply to a greeting; if they did so at all it was unwillingly and almost to themselves. Even Father Prudente, still naïvely expecting some demonstration of respect, got nothing but a stare; he was unable to decide whether the look was rude or astonished.

The children were often victimized by the strangers. Mandoví, a young boy who sold cigarettes from a shoe box, was constantly being provoked. The first time, taking the men for possible customers, he approached them and offered his wares. One of the men waved him away, but the other one wished to know what was in the box. But instead of asking to see, as anyone would who was new in town, he just took off the lid and dropped it onto the ground without so much as a grunt. Mandoví was displeased and angrily snatched the box out of the man's reach and bent down to pick up the lid, wondering whether he should pay any further heed to that kind of person or just turn away. When he straightened up, rubbing the lid on his clothes to get the dust off, he felt himself grasped by the collar while another hand took the box away from him.

What could he do, small and scrawny as he was, against two enormous men with bearded faces?

The man held the box against his ribs, and with his right

73

hand picked out the largest bundle of home-made cigarettes.

"And what's this?" he asked, as if he didn't know, turning the bundle this way and that and not looking at the boy.

Mandoví would have liked to say that it was peanut brittle or sausage rolls, but he found the patience to explain properly. The man was not interested in his reply, and was already trying to bite the thread that held the bundle together.

"Don't take it off, they'll all spill out on the ground," Mandoví warned, but too late; the man had bitten through the thread, and the cigarettes, freed of their bonds, opened like a flower and scattered on the ground.

"Now pay. You undid them, you pay for them," said Mandoví, thinking he was applying a logic that anyone would understand. But the man let out a guffaw that shook his whole body, and dropped the box. It fell on its side and spilled out all the remaining bundles.

Mandoví waited for the man to stop laughing but, when it became obvious that this would be some time, he seized the opportunity to pick up the bundles that were still whole. He left the loose cigarettes because in his mind they had ceased to belong to him. Still laughing, the man started to stagger around like a drunkard, stepping on the cigarettes, crushing the little bundles, ruining the box. Mandoví stopped with his two small hands still on the ground; he looked up and saw four legs—scaffolding, shuddering mobile beams—walking away.

Without stopping to think, he picked up sticks, stones, corncobs, and threw them blindly, furiously, the thuds echoing dully as they landed. He screamed at them but the men ran off and the stones fell short.

When he arrived home, Mandoví thought someone had suddenly become ill, or that his father had hurt himself in his workshop. There were a lot of people on the porch talking, asking questions, venturing opinions. Mandoví entered in some trepidation, and his mother ran to embrace him.

"Son! How did you come to do such a thing?"

His father left a group talking together in front of the window, and said sternly to the boy:

"Mandoví, come with me to the shop."

Mandoví put what remained of the box of cigarettes on the table and looked at his mother, paying no attention to the others gathered there. His father called him again, and he followed him down the small stairway into the backyard.

Nobody made a move to leave; if Seu Apolinario chose to punish his son, they wanted the satisfaction of hearing him yell. His mother went to the front window to avoid hearing him, and hoped her husband would not be too hard on the boy; after all, what boy doesn't misbehave now and then? A neighbor woman tried to console her but she did not hear the soft words; her attention was concentrated on the workshop at the side of the house—it would not be long now before Mandoví would be crying out as each blow landed. Beating the boy, Apolinario

75

neither restrained himself nor chose where the lash would fall, and he would insist on beating with that leather strap, so thick and hard . . .

The neighbor kept talking, and the mother became impatient: the shrieks did not come; something out of the ordinary was happening.

It was quite a shock when Mandoví appeared beside her ready to explain about the cigarettes.

"Did you tell your father?" she asked, after hearing him out.

"Yes, ma'am."

"And he didn't do anything?"

"No, ma'am. He said I did right."

His mother's relief was born and died right there at the window. It died when she understood the reason for so many visitors: all of them expected some sort of retaliation from the strangers and they had come to see it. The two men were not going meekly home after being stoned in the street. And Apolinario's support of Mandoví had made the situation worse; when the strangers heard that he had not been punished, they themselves would want to punish him, and who could tell how they would do it?

The house was filled with people the rest of the day. Some got tired and went home, but others came to take their place; everybody in town presented himself on the small porch, as if coming to kiss the hand of the Almighty on a feast day. Noisily, they bumped against the furniture, almost knocking over the water jar set on a high stand in the corner (someone had to put it straight every minute or so but each time a little of the water spilled over, making mud of the floor), people stepped on each other's feet, excused themselves, and stepped again. Finally Apolinario could stand it no longer and decided to end the hullabaloo. He clapped his hands to get everyone's attention and asked them all to go home. He said that no one had died yet, thank God, and they should go and occupy their time with a little hard work, just as he had been doing since quite early that day—and he went around picking up hats that were on pegs, on the table, on the windowsill, in the hands of their owners, placed them on the visitors' heads (often the wrong hat on the wrong head), and pushed the people out through the passageway, holding out his arms to stop the ones that threatened to come back.

Even though his wife thought it was a good idea, she was a bit ashamed because among those asked to leave were a few of her personal friends, who could find no excuse for staying after Apolinario had had his say.

"So now they know, the wise guys! And you can make supper in peace," Apolinario told his wife. "If you need me, I'll be in the shop. And something else, Serena. It might be better if we didn't let Mandoví go out again today."

Dona Serena approved of her husband's courageous and confident manner, but she wondered if he might be just a little too cocky in the face of danger. Mulling it over and over, she became careless in the kitchen and committed one housewifely error after another—she burned her hand on a saucepan, she let the rice get sticky, she forgot the

77

kettle until it boiled over and almost put out the fire. Dona Serena could not get the men from the compound, or the evils they might be capable of, out of her mind.

When Apolinario came in to dinner she told him very tactfully that it would be better if he also did not leave the house that night.

"Why not? I don't have to be careful."

"I'm frightened because of what Mandoví did."

"There's nothing to be scared of. They asked for it."

"But suppose the men want revenge?"

"They won't. If any of them comes around here with a chip on his shoulder, I'll knock it off."

Instead of being soothed by her husband's bravado, Dona Serena felt even more alarmed.

"Now, be careful, Apolinario. I'm really scared."

"There's no reason to be. A man who's right has no need of fright."

"Well, I hope so."

But Apolinario sacrificed his evening stroll after all. When it got dark he went to his shop, picked out one of the lighter sledge hammers, and brought it into the house. While Mandoví fetched water from the well to fill the jars and Dona Serena scraped corn husks for the ciga- rettes, he leaned out the window, smoking and replying to the "good evenings" of passersby. Afterward he went onto the porch and lay stiffly in his hammock, the sledge hammer within easy reach. That night Mandoví was not allowed to play in the square.

"But, mother . . . what harm will it do?"

"You'd better not. You can miss today. There's no law that you have to play games."

"If I see them coming, I'll run. No one can beat me running."

"I don't want you to go unless your father gives you permission."

Called on to give his opinion, Apolinario backed his wife.

"You're not going. Your mother has already told you and that's that. Pick up a book and go study."

There was no hope. It was indeed a wasted night for Mandoví.

It LOOKED AS IF the danger was over. Mandoví went on selling cigarettes, against Dona Serena's wishes, and there were no disagreeable incidents; once he passed close to some of the men but they either did not see him or were not interested.

Then one day, on his way to the beach to fill his wagon, Geminiano stopped at the workshop with a message for Apolinario: he was to present himself at the compound.

Apolinario stopped the bellows in order to hear better. "What's that?"

"You're to go to the compound. They sent for you."

Apolinario came toward the door, wiping off his hands. "Why should I go to the compound?"

"I really don't know. They asked me to give you the message, and I'm giving it."

Apolinario looked at Geminiano seated on his wagon, playing half-heartedly with the whip, quite evidently to avoid looking him in the eye; he felt a mixture of pity and contempt and, thinking a bit, decided to keep only the pity.

"Thank you for your trouble, Gemi. I don't have anything to do there. I discuss new jobs right here in my shop."

"They don't want to order anything. They just want to talk to you."

"That makes it worse. If it isn't to discuss a job, then I have even less intention of going."

Geminiano feigned interest in the handle of his whip, as if it were something he were seeing for the first time; finally he cleared his throat and spoke.

"If I were you, I'd go."

"Then *you* go. I'm not going."

Geminiano thought a while, and stopped insisting.

"Well, I delivered the message. What shall I say in return?"

"Say you delivered the message."

Geminiano started off down the street in his cart, and Apolinario went back to his bellows. The more he thought about the message, the more annoyed he became. The nerve people had these days! A man is at peace in his own little corner and along comes some meddler with an impudent message. If he had cheese to sell, he should take it to the cheese buyers. Here was one man who was not going to that compound; first because he was no dog to answer someone's whistle and, second, because if the men wanted to complain about Mandoví, the talk could end in an argument, maybe even a fight, and when one fights in another man's corner he loses the advantage of being right.

Apolinario had not intended to say anything at home but when he arrived for lunch, he realized that the matter was no secret. Dona Serena was waiting for him.

"What are you going to do, Apolinario?"

"What am I going to do? I'm going to wash my hands and then feed my stomach."

"I don't think that's funny. I mean about the message Geminiano brought."

"Ah, the message. It's gone."

"What do you mean?"

"I got the message and I sent it back."

She bit her lip, waiting; when she realized that he was not going to explain further, she spoke.

"I've been thinking . . ."

Busy washing his hands in the basin at the corner of the porch, he considered himself excused from asking what she had been thinking. If a man has to take into account all a woman's fears . . .

"We could go and spend a few days at my brother's farm until things get quiet again."

Apolinario dried his hands, sat down at the table, picked up a fork with crooked tines, and busied himself with straightening them.

"Please say yes," she begged.

"No."

She was alarmed at the roughness of his reply but, in the silence that followed, she calmed down and pursued: "It's dangerous to stay here, Apolinario."

He threw down the fork and spoke impatiently.

"There's no sense in it, Serena. Why should we dig ourselves into some little farm in the middle of nowhere? I didn't kill anyone, I didn't steal. And I don't like the country, you know I don't like it."

"It's a small sacrifice. I don't even like to leave the house, I hardly ever go out in the street. But I know that here I won't have any peace."

"There's no sense in it. Aren't I here, whatever happens?"

"But there are so many of them, Apolinario. And I'm so afraid."

"There's no danger. What they needed was someone to stand up to them, and I did. If they need any more, I'm the man for the job. And now we better have lunch. Where is the boy? He'd better break that habit of being late for meals!"

Dona Serena leaned out the window, shouted toward the yard for Mandoví, and went to see about lunch. It was eaten in silence.

When he had finished, Apolinario rinsed out his mouth with water from the jar, spat it out onto the wall to avoid wetting the floor, and returned to his workshop whistling.

That afternoon Manuel Florencio visited Apolinario. Manuel needed a wedge for the blade of his plane; he gave the measurements, said he was in no hurry. He tried to draw Apolinario out.

"Lot of work, Apolinario?"

"Plenty. And you?"

"Enough. Lots of repairs." Manuel glanced around. "And lots of troubles, too."

"That's something we've all got. Nobody goes without. Father Prudente says it's all because of Adam's fall."

"Yeah, but some have more than others."

"It only seems so. Actually, we've all got the same."

Manuel watched him, waiting for him to go on. Apolinario spread some more charcoal on the fire, used the bellows. He appeared not to want to talk.

"A while ago something happened to me . . ." said Manuel. "Did you hear about it?"

"Didn't hear a thing. Spend most of my time in here without much need to hear things."

Manuel leaned on the anvil block, crossed his legs, folded his arms, and told Apolinario the story of the wagon repair. When he had finished, Apolinario puffed a few more times with the bellows and raked the coals.

"Well, that's something I would not do," he said at last. "You can be sure of one thing— I won't do forced labor."

Manuel smiled sadly, unhappy because he could not say the same. He used to think that way, but he had had to give in. How long could Apolinario hold out?

"You don't know those men, Apolinario. They get all around you, put on the squeeze, keep you on a treadmill. You'll see."

Apolinario glanced at him quickly, suspiciously. Did he too know of the message?

"They'd be wasting their time with me. My trade is hammering iron."

Manuel thought of his own trade, cutting wood, and compared the two materials. Would the difference between them have any effect on the resistance of people working with them? No, that would be nonsense. Wood is wood, iron is iron; and people are people. Whether a man turns out to be a blacksmith or a carpenter or a cobbler depends entirely on chance, as it did in his own case. His father had been a carpenter, and Manuel had learned the trade to help out; he couldn't spend his time just fooling around doing nothing. It was probably the same with Apolinario. But did the strength of the vocation have anything to do with it? A lot of boys had wanted to learn carpentering with him; they fiddled, messed about, and gave up, never even learning to hold the tools properly.

Could it be that the habit of working always with the same material, year in year out, influences the soul of the man, infecting him with softness or strength? If you looked hard enough, it seemed as if each person began to resemble the trade he followed.

Thinking about this, he peered at Apolinario. A full face, square, firm-fleshed, it looked as if it had been put together in sections, each piece hammered in by force; a wide forehead, with bumps on each side like imbedded swellings; a big nose, well buried in his face; small eyes not taking up too much space; wide chin, the tip turned

84

upward; neck almost as big around as his head. Apolinario's face could never be the face of a tinsmith, for example. A typical tinsmith was João José, small, ratty, narrowshouldered like a boy, tiny hands (you don't have to be big to cut tin because it's so pliable). João José, all rolled up and shiny, grumbling, snapping and scratching at people.

And he, himself? Soft as wood being tooled? Feigning toughness at times, like knots that the tool pays no heed to, passing over them and planing them level? A carpenter's hands, his body, his soul, must not be tougher than the wood he handles. Wood cannot be shaped by hitting it hard, in anger; only a woodsman does that, but a woodsman resembles the ax which he swings without mercy and without consideration. All one has to do is look at the face of a woodsman to see that he lacks gentleness or tact; he does not need it.

A blacksmith also works with hammer blows, using brute force. But there is a difference: he has measurements to follow, a goal to reach, an idea to shape; he does not hammer to cut or to shatter, but to flatten and form. A blacksmith works to make, not to undo; if he undoes, it is to remake. There is a hidden delicacy in the strength of a blacksmith.

Manuel looked once more at Apolinario, and noting the gentleness of his strong hands, he breathed easier. Apolinario would cause a lot of trouble before he gave in, and he might never give in. It would be a very good thing, because those men really needed a lesson.

85

"Be careful with them, Apolinario. They like to have their own way."

"Don't worry. They won't get it with me."

Manuel was glad to hear that. It was almost a guarantee that the men would not be having a picnic in Apolinario's backyard.

"When can I come by to get my plane?"

"It'll be ready today. If I go out tonight, I'll leave it at your house."

Manuel said good-bye and went away happy. Apolinario was going to give those men some trouble.

Passing by Amancio's store, he found the same subject at boiling point.

"Geminiano said he didn't get angry at all. Just said he wasn't going."

"It wasn't just that. He sent back another message saying the distance was the same, coming or going."

"He'll be sorry. The examples are there to see. Look at Geminiano. What do you think, Manuel Florencio?"

Manuel did not reply at once. First he found a place to lean against.

"I don't think Apolinario is going to give in."

"Did you speak to him?"

"No. It's my own opinion."

Nobody said anything for some time, everyone dwelling on the consequences of a second refusal from Apolinario— because one thing was sure, the men were not going to let the matter lie. Finally one of them spoke.

"He'll be like all the others—start out tough, but end up turning soft. Isn't that so, Amancio?"

86

Taking the question as criticism of his own conduct, Amancio answered coldly.

"Each man knows himself."

They all shrank back a little, fearing a violent reaction; but Amancio, who was filling a bottle of kerosene for a small boy, busied himself with tin can, funnel, and bottle, and said no more. One of the men tried to help him but, being inexperienced, left no air space between the funnel and the neck of the bottle and the kerosene splashed on the counter and on the would-be helper's hand.

"Look out, you fool!" Amancio shouted.

The man became even more confused, lifting the funnel completely, and the rest of the kerosene spilled all over the counter, frothing up between the fibers of the old wood.

"Now clean it up!" ordered Amancio.

"With what?" asked the man, embarrassed and frustrated.

"I don't know. How about your tongue?"

The others laughed, hoping to placate Amancio. Amancio laughed too and, when he was satisfied, directed:

"It serves you right for butting in. Go in and get an old sack."

The man went in the back and returned with a bunch of rags; in order to avoid another mistake, he first asked if those particular rags might be used. Without looking, Amancio told him to clean up the mess quickly.

After that no one cared to continue the conversation. Instead they all tried to think of some way to leave the store naturally; when Amancio was in a bad mood, the best thing to do was to leave him alone. When Manuel

Florencio got up and stretched and said he would be getting along, the others all found that they too had to go.

THE DAYS PASSED and Apolinario was not bothered. Geminiano continued his journeys up and down the street on his wagon and, if he saw the blacksmith at the door, he shouted a greeting and went on his way as if nothing had happened—Apolinario acknowledged him with a nod or a wave and continued his work. Dona Serena began to calm down and said nothing more about going to the country, coming to the conclusion that her idea had probably been a silly one. In Amancio's store, in the shops, in the streets, Apolinario was pointed out as a man of stature, an example to them all. It was said that if there had been half a dozen more men like him in Manirema, the men in the compound would not have dared bully anyone.

The workshop began to be frequented by townspeople hoping to catch a little more courage by talking to a brave man. Apolinario wondered why they were so lacking in things to do; he spoke very little except to state that he had done nothing out of the ordinary, that he had merely put a stop to insolence—which, after all, is a man's duty if he wants to keep his self-respect. He talked without interrupting his work, not wanting his shop to turn into a meeting place like Amancio's store. Moreover, many customers were now ordering locks, bars, and roasting spits, as if they were great novelties.

One day Geminiano again stopped his wagon at the

door, called Apolinario, and handed him a piece of paper, folded in four, with Apolinario's name written on one side. Apolinario found the absence of an envelope peculiar. Everyone gets letters inside envelopes; did they consider him not worth the waste of one? He took the paper, turned it over in his dirty hand, but did not open it.

"It's delivered."

"Aren't you going to read it?"

"Not now. I'll wait until I have nothing else to do."

"But I have orders . . ." Geminiano said, somewhat discomfited.

"I said it was delivered. When I have time, I'll read it," Apolinario replied, and went back in without further ado.

"Then I'll stop in on the way back," Geminiano shouted, thwarted but still insistent.

"You can if you want to. But I'm in no hurry to read it."

Apolinario left the paper under a piece of iron and turned his attention to a saddle frame he had promised for that day; all it needed was bending and fastening the back arc—the front one and the four crossbars were ready.

Saddle frames might not seem like much, but they're not a simple matter at all. If the arcs are bent too far inward, the saddle will not fit properly on the horse's back; it will sit high and the weight of the rider will force it down, making sores on the animal; if the arcs are not bent enough, the saddle comes down too far and the horse's backbone suffers.

Apolinario heated the iron and set about bending it very slowly, constantly comparing it with the wooden model already proven and much praised by all his customers. He was still bending the last portion, preparing it for fastening on the last crossbar, when Geminiano returned from the river. Apolinario had already forgotten the letter, but when he saw Geminiano he remembered.

"Oh, your paper. Would you believe I still haven't looked at it?"

Irritated at his indifference, Geminiano told him:

"It's an important matter, Apolinario. You don't seem to understand."

Now Apolinario was the one to get annoyed. Throwing hammer and frame aside, not caring whether it came undone or not, he stalked to the door and said loudly:

"The only thing that's important to me is my work. When I feel like it, I'll open it and read it. Will that do? If it will, fine. If not, take it back. I won't miss it."

"I can't take it back. They sent it to you and they're waiting for your answer."

"Waiting, are they? Then let them pull up a chair and sit down. Right now I've no intention of reading any kind of paper."

"Think it over, Apolinario. You're borrowing trouble. They're already angry at you."

"Well, they're going to be angrier. Watch."

Apolinario stamped back into his workshop, picked up the folded paper, threw it on the coals, and gave the fire several blasts from the bellows. The paper withered a little, writhed, yellowed, began to smoke. A loud puff and a single flame ended its existence.

From the top of the wagon Geminiano craned his neck

to see what was happening but could not because it was dark in the shop.

"What did you do?" he asked when Apolinario came back to the door.

"I burned it."

"Burned it? Without reading it? Now you've done it!" He shook his head from side to side as if he were witnessing a hopeless tragedy. "Apolinario, now you're in real trouble." He stared at Apolinario with sorrow in his eyes, wakened Serrote, and departed still shaking his head.

Apolinario finished the frame and hung it on a nail in the wall to await its owner and, at the same time, be admired by the passersby until it was picked up. A blacksmith's job has its odd side. Often quite some time passes without his making a certain item; then one day someone comes into the shop and wants, for example, a front-door lock. The blacksmith makes it, the owner does not come to fetch it right away, and it hangs in the shop. All of a sudden every passerby notices it and wants to buy it. Because it is already sold, they order one just like it and the blacksmith spends a whole season making nothing else. Considering this, Apolinario decided to postpone his other jobs and make two or three more saddle frames to take advantage of the interest he knew would be forthcoming.

He was washing his hands at the barrel when Amancio arrived. He came in and noticed the saddle frame at once: a good way to start the conversation.

"Rather special, that frame. Very well balanced. It is for sale?"

"No. It's an order."

"Hmm. Whose?"

"A man from Brumado."

"Hmm. It's first-class."

Having praised the frame, Amancio thought it time to plunge in.

"Apolinario, you hadn't the right to do it."

Drying his hands on a worn-out shirt, Apolinario answered him calmly.

"If I did it, it was because I had the right. It's when you don't have the right that you don't do something."

"Don't start in with your philosophy. You had no right to do it."

"But I did it. Now what?"

"Now I'm obliged to come here and smooth things over."

"Who obliged you? I didn't."

Amancio searched for patience in a deep sigh and tried again.

"You behaved very badly. The men sent you a message, do you think you can just pick it up and burn it without reading it? Where was your head? An insult like that, to them, of all people!"

"Why are you burning up? You're acting like you were inside the paper!"

Realizing that he was getting nowhere, Amancio tried another tack.

"You don't have to be so afraid of them. Actually, they haven't done anyone any harm. They're polite, they know how to say things without offending. You could go there, talk it over, explain yourself."

Apolinario was beginning to find Amancio's insistence amusing, so he did not get angry.

"Amancio, I don't want to judge you because I don't know where your shoe pinches. But I don't have to fawn on anyone and I have nothing to explain. They can wait until hell freezes over before they will get me to go and see them. If they want to come here and talk straight, I'll lend an ear; but if they come with demands, out they go."

Amancio picked up the sledge hammer that was on the anvil block; he examined it, weighed it in his hands, put it down.

"Apolinario, I'm your friend. That's why I'm taking the time. You won't lose anything by going to them. But if you are stubborn, things can only get worse. They're patient, but everybody's patience comes to an end. You could go there while there is still time, explain yourself, and be free of it. There's no need for a detailed explanation; just say you got careless and the wind blew the message into the fire. You've got a family; think of them and don't do anything foolish."

Apolinario walked around the anvil, came up close to Amancio, and looked him in the eye.

"Amancio, you have the reputation of being a fighting man. I haven't; I've never done any fighting. But one thing I'll tell you—I won't throw in the sponge until I see where I'm throwing it. I don't surrender at the drop of a hat. If you came here as their spokesman, go back to them with my answer."

Amancio stared at the ground, frustrated. He had not

liked the reference to his fighting, especially mixed with the sly hint about throwing in the sponge; but he was on a diplomatic mission and could not afford to lose his temper.

"You're getting upset over nothing, Apolinario. They like to settle their differences in a friendly way. Look at Geminiano and Manuel Florencio. So far, the men haven't done anyone any harm."

"Because everyone's bowed down to them. It's enough for the men to want something and everybody hands it over, shivering in their boots."

Amancio was silent, scraping the floor with the toe of his boot. He looked sadly at Apolinario and tried to justify himself.

"People can't always do what they want. You'll find out." He went to the door and turned around. "So you're really not going?"

"No, I'm not," Apolinario told him drily.

Amancio departed defeated, but basically he seemed pleased—at least that was what could be deduced from his confident, cheerful step.

IN A TOWN without secrets, news jumps fences, penetrates walls, leaps from window to window, from mouth to ear, with great speed and ceaseless chattering. On a very hot day, when the whole population goes indoors and outside there is only the sun glinting on the stones and the white walls, if someone in the street bends down to pick something up, the whole town knows that so-and-so found

a coin or some valuable object. Everyone lives continually
exposed to watchful eyes that feign a total lack of interest.
That was the way it was in Manirema.

Before Apolinario had even finished his dinner, the
whole town was aware of the burned message and the
home truths told to Amancio. Why Amancio failed to strike
back was a subject for much conjecture. What could be
the reason for the change in Amancio, and in such a short
time? And why his interest in the squabble between Apolinario and the men? Had he taken Apolinario's side it would
have been more easily understood; but to take the part of
the men, counsel Apolinario to surrender, press him to the
men's advantage—it left the townspeople bewildered and
mistrustful. Once before, when the dogs came, Amancio's
behavior had been severely censured. He had not only
considered the invasion of the animals amusing; but he
had jeered at people trying to chase them away. That was
not all: when the crisis had passed he had gone about
asking questions, apparently trying to find out who had
been most unkind to the dogs. But if he were siding with
the men in the hope of some reward, all indications were
that he was wasting his time. No one knew of any special consideration shown him; he had not even been
able to embark on the much-touted enlargement of the
store.

In the evening, just before the lamps were lit, two men
entered the store. They entered without a greeting, neither
word nor gesture, and stood staring at the customers gathered there. All talk stopped at once, as it does in school

95

when the kids are all fooling around and the teacher suddenly walks in.

"Where's the owner?" one of them inquired, looking at no one in particular, while the other turned to look at the sky.

"Seu Amancio is inside."

"He must have gone in the back."

"He'll be right out."

Having received three eager-to-please replies, the man issued his order.

"Get him."

All three informants rose at once and rushed to the back of the store, tripping over each other at the tiny door in the counter, shouting Amancio's name. Moments later the four returned, Amancio fastening his belt.

"Ah, yes, gentlemen. I had to go inside for a minute," Amancio apologized.

The men made no comment, probably considering this detail unworthy of their attention; the important thing was that Amancio should not keep them waiting. One of them turned toward the customers, who had already resumed their seats on the burlap bags and crates with the obvious intention of staying, and asked:

"Have you gentlemen already made your purchases?"

They understood and began to leave, as disappointed as children excluded from the company of grown-ups. Just then the lamps came on and Amancio wished those present a good evening; the men merely nodded their heads, and one of them made a sign to Amancio to close the store.

The store was under surveillance, of course. Several people had noticed when the men arrived, and now they saw Amancio leave hurriedly, his coat slung across his back, his arms jerkily seeking for the sleeves. Coming to the conclusion that he was going to fetch Apolinario, the townspeople followed him quietly, keeping a safe distance in order to have a disclaimer ready in case they were seen. Knowing the Amancio of old, they did not care to be caught without a plausible excuse.

Apolinario was at the old dovecote corner, passing the time of day with friends, when Amancio rushed by with the look of a man about to cut his father down from the scaffold.

"He didn't even say 'Good evening.' Where could he be going?" wondered one.

"I bet he's on his way to my house," said Apolinario, undisturbed.

"Then let's call him back," suggested another, dying to know the reason for Amancio's haste.

"Not me. Let him waste his time. He makes enough money."

"Well, I'm going to call him. Amancio! Apolinario's here!"

Amancio stopped, hesitated a moment, and turned back. The light at the corner was weak and Apolinario was standing in the shadow of the lamppost. Amancio came closer, frowning and squinting.

"What if I was a snake, eh, Amancio?" Apolinario teased, coming out of the shadow.

97

Amancio pretended not to understand and, ignoring the presence of the others, ordered:

"You come with me. There are people at the store waiting to talk to you. Hurry up."

The others came closer, afraid of missing Apolinario's reply.

"Who are they? What do they want to talk about?"

"Oh, Apolinario! The men. They sent for you."

"Are they crippled or something? Can't they come here?"

"Don't be like that, Apolinario. I mean it. I came to get you. Hurry up, because they're waiting for you. Don't be afraid."

Apolinario dug his feet into the ground, slammed clenched fists into his pockets, and said angrily:

"Amancio, I don't want any trouble with you. My differences have nothing to do with you. If you think I'm scared, go tell them I'm shaking with fear. But I refuse to go to them because of the sheer impertinence of it. I will receive them in my shop or in my house or even here, if it's urgent. But I won't go to a place where they are waiting. Did you ever hear anything like it? They've got it into their heads that I'm to present myself like a common soldier in front of the commander. I don't see it that way. I have no commander. The idea!"

"See?" Amancio appealed to the others. "The men want to talk to him, they came all the way from the compound on foot, they send for him politely, and Apolinario gets like this. What are they going to think?"

"What does it have to do with you, Amancio?" one of them answered. "You're acting like their nursemaid. I'm surprised at you. Leave Apolinario here and them over there, and get out of the middle."

"They asked me to do it. I'm just trying to be helpful. I came to give him the message. It's nothing to make a fuss about."

"Well, you gave him the message. You've dumped your load. Now you can wash your hands of it," said Apolinario, ending the matter.

But Amancio would not give up. He had left the store to summon Apolinario. How could he go back and say that Apolinario had refused the invitation? Those men were hard-headed; they could get angry and send him back here to fetch Apolinario any way he could. But how? Dead or alive? No, they wouldn't do that. Why should they? But they did want Apolinario at the store. That much was certain. Amancio simply could not return without him. How would he face them?

"I'm surprised at you, Apolinario. We've always been friends. Remember when you were in bed with pneumonia and I gave you all your supplies on the cuff? Now that I need you, you back off. Do you think you can only get a stomach ache once?"

It was true. Amancio had been extremely decent at a very difficult time; but what right did he have to bring it up now? When he had been sick, Apolinario had been hard-pressed; Dona Serena's cigarettes brought in nothing. They had been reduced to selling one thing one day,

99

another the next—earrings, a gold chain, even a small saint's image. When they were just about to part with their wedding bands, Amancio had appeared, had chided them and said he would be very angry indeed if Apolinario did not get everything he needed from the store. It was a fine gesture, and Apolinario recognized it. Now Amancio was asking to be paid in another coin. Well, if it had to be like that . . .

"All right, Amancio, I'll go. I owe, I pay. There can't be any doubt about that."

Having won out, Amancio realized what he had done and wanted to make amends.

"I'm not asking because of the credit I gave you. If you ever need it, I'll do it again. I was just asking you a favor in the name of our friendship."

"I understand you, Amancio. One hand washes the other, isn't that it?"

Amancio knew that no real victory had been won; on the contrary, he regretted the colors he had shown in front of the others. And it was all because of those men, damn them for their sins. Why could he not have behaved as Apolinario had done? Now he was also responsible for the defeat of Apolinario.

Walking beside Apolinario, who had said good-bye to his friends and started out ahead of him, Amancio looked as if he were the one being taken to the meeting against his will. When they reached the store, it was Apolinario who pushed open the door.

The two strangers were sitting on the counter, dangling

their legs. With knives taken from Amancio's stock, one was working on a can of quince paste open in his lap, and the other on a cheese held tight between his arm and his left side. Exchanging slices on the knife points, they joined cheese to quince paste and ate with great relish; even the crumbled cheese falling onto laps and boots was gathered up and eaten, so eager were they not to miss anything. The appearance of Amancio and Apolinario did not interrupt them, they merely glanced up and went on eating. At last one of the men asked, his mouth still full:

"Want a hunk? Here, eat it. First-class."

Apolinario shook his head resolutely. Amancio hesitated, was about to accept out of politeness, but the other stranger stopped him.

"He's the owner. He can eat it any time he wants. This is for us."

Amancio watched silently as the men ate. Apolinario went over to a corner, picked up a handful of beans from an open bag, tossed them into his mouth, and peeled them with his teeth. The sound seemed to annoy one of the men; he kept glancing reprovingly at Apolinario and finally, realizing that he would not take a hint, shouted:

"Stop that! It sounds like a rat."

Apolinario was so taken aback by the rebuke that he did not know what to do. However, watching the man disguisedly and seeing him again busy paring a slice off the cheese, he decided the man had not really meant it, had been trying to be funny; especially as Amancio was laughing and imitating the nervous chewing of the agouti,

101

with the obvious intention of buttering up the strangers. So Apolinario took the joke in good humor and, to prove that he had not minded, continued to chew, a little louder this time.

The men finished eating, wiped the knives and their hands on their trousers (Amancio said there was no need to clean the knives, leave them, he would wash them later), and remained seated on the counter, swinging their legs and running their tongues along their teeth to clean them.

Apolinario waited for them to speak. He had come to hear what they had to say, but they remained silent, digesting their snack. Could they have changed their minds, or were they employing the time to organize their attack? Apolinario stretched and yawned a defiant yawn —and even then the men did not move.

Amancio decided to take the initiative.

"This is Apolinario, the smithy we were talking about. He agreed to come . . ."

The men looked at each other, irritated, then at Amancio, but did not glance even once at Apolinario. One of them ran his hand through his hair and suggested:

"You talk to him, Neiva."

"Why me? You do it."

"You insisted on this. Now talk."

Apolinario seated himself on a sack of beans, folded his arms. and waited for them to come to a decision. The man called Neiva took a deep breath, like someone getting ready to dive, and started to speak, but was prevented by the discovery of something lodged between his teeth, requiring immediate attention. He asked Amancio for a matchstick, whittled it meticulously with a knife, and poked out the offending scrap—a quince seed, to be sure —and then took advantage of the occasion to make sure all his teeth were clean, seeming to forget about Apolinario.

Outside the shop the whispers of the many who had hurried to the store after them could be heard. They were trying desperately to make out some of the conversation. Neiva finished picking his teeth, snapped the matchstick neatly in two, spit one piece out, and chewed thoughtfully on the other. Finally he began.

"Yes sir, Seu Apolinario. As you know, we came to this place for a short visit. But we might just decide to stay on."

Apolinario was listening impassively but made some involuntary movement with his head, which the man took for affirmation.

"You knew that, didn't you? Yes. Well, since that's the way things are, we are taking steps to make our job here easier."

Apolinario took care to make no other movement. The man was having trouble explaining, and he was not going to help him out. He only wanted to know where he fitted into their plans.

"As you know, and our Amancio here knows too, we've come from a long way off. You might say we're rolling stones. That's why we have to tread so carefully and not step in anyone else's pumpkin patch."

"Isn't that what I said?" interrupted Amancio. "What did I tell you?"

"We have done everything to avoid misunderstandings and arguments; that sort of thing only serves to make enemies."

Apolinario said nothing, determined not to speak before the time was ripe.

"We already know that you are a sensible, serious, hard-working man. You stay that way; you're on the right path."

Apolinario thought the advice idiotic but did not say so. He kept quiet to avoid compromising himself, pretending that the man was speaking of some other person. The man gazed at the floor, snapped his fingers, ran his hand through his hair again.

"How old are you?" he asked suddenly.

The question worried Apolinario. What could his age possibly have to do with the subject at hand? Well, no matter.

"Forty-one," he answered reluctantly.

"And your boy?"

"Ten. Nine or ten. His mother keeps track."

"Does he know his tables yet?"

The other man shook his head and spoke through a yawn.

"You're stretching it out too much."

"You've got your system, I've got mine. Please don't annoy me," Neiva answered.

"You're not getting anywhere. Instead of coming straight to the point, you're pecking around it."

"Will you stop it? Are you going to let me get on with the job?" Neiva asked, looking hard at the other.

The other man leaned toward Amancio, smiled sarcastically, and said:

"He wants to get on with the job. He thinks he knows how. How, my foot!"

Instead of getting angry, as Amancio and Apolinario had feared, Neiva smiled.

"Careful, or I'll tell them your nickname. If you make me angry, I'll tell," he warned.

The other blinked hurriedly to hide his discomfiture, swallowed hard, and fell back. Neiva, victorious, needled him.

"He has such a peculiar nickname, haven't you, Chaves?"

The other man remained silent, head buried deep in his shoulders, staring straight ahead. Neiva suddenly thrust his hand inside his shirt, caught something in his fingers, and brought it out; he looked at it closely, rubbed his fingers together, and wiped them on his trousers.

"Where are you from, Seu Apolinario? Are you from here?"

The one called Chaves shook his head and clucked his tongue several times. Neiva looked at him, thought a while, and asked him:

"Do you want to say something? Go ahead, you have my permission."

"It's all wrong," said Chaves. "That question comes at the end. See that, Seu Amancio? Didn't I say he was no good at the job?"

105

"Then why'd you push it off on me?"

"To watch you get yourself mixed up. Stop showing off."

"Is that so? Then I won't ask another question. The interrogation is finished, so there! Seu Apolinario, you can go now. On my say-so."

Apolinario stared at them and forced himself to smother a wild desire to laugh. No reason to get too familiar with these fools. Laughter is to share only with friends. With strangers one must be formal.

"Then, good night," said Apolinario, without looking at anyone in particular.

Amancio looked about quickly, picked out a tin of cookies, and pushed it into Apolinario's hands as he reached the door.

"Take them to the boy. He likes them, doesn't he?"

Apolinario glanced at the gift and decided to accept it in return for the waste of his time; as he stepped outside he heard the door slam and the argument explode inside. Amancio was begging for quiet. In spite of his fatigue and irritation at being subjected to such nonsense, Apolinario could not resist the urge to laugh. He let out a guffaw that resounded down the alley, not caring in the least that it might be heard inside the store.

SOME PEOPLE took no interest at all in the men from the compound, or at least seemed to think that they could live without them. Pedrinho Afonso was one. At work the whole day in Seu Quinel's store, he overheard what one or another said about the strangers, but he was neither impressed nor interested. He knew there were some mysterious men about, outsiders who were doing some sort of construction work that no one could figure out. Occasionally he saw some of them in the street and, at first, said a mannerly "Good day"; but he soon gave that up. Those ill-bred persons had no attraction for him: first of all because he had no time to run after them like some people, and besides that there was Nazaré, a very serious and absorbing interest. Two or three times a day Nazaré discovered some pretext to pass by the store and glance quickly inside. Sometimes she even came in to buy ribbon or buttons, or to see if there was any more fabric like the sample she carried, but she was rarely waited on by Pedrinho (which really did not make too much difference because he was very discreet indeed in front of Seu Quinel and the customers). In any case, they saw each other, and that was enough to make the whole day worthwhile.

When Nazaré departed from the shop, she left behind a pleasant odor of cleanliness and a babble of comments from the customers. One of them would bring up the fact that she semed ready for marriage; another that a marriage in Manirema would be difficult to arrange unless it were with someone from another town; a third hinted at a less conventional solution with a traveling salesman, citing well-known precedents. Pedrinho always got very red and, to hide it, went to do something or other at the back of the store, or pretend that he did.

The courtship continued without any real encounters,

fed only by those bashful half-meetings in the shop and by glances exchanged in the evenings after prayers, when Nazaré returned from church with her godmother and passed the dovecote corner where Pedrinho always stood watch with a group of boys. Nazaré would look shyly at him and smile a hidden smile, and Pedrinho knew they were still courting.

There were more open courtships in the town, ones that included walks on the bridge at night, long conversations at garden gates, and apparently accidental meetings in poorly frequented places. Nazaré and Pedrinho were aware of these but it was not up to them to modify a courtship that had begun with much difficulty and which was very closely watched, very often hindered.

But one day, at *jabuticaba** time, everything changed with no effort at all. It was Sunday and Pedrinho was walking on the road between the garden fences and the riverbank when he caught sight of the loaded *jabuticabeira* trees in Nazaré's garden. There was certainly no shortage of *jabuticabas* anywhere, but these were too tempting to resist. If the gate wasn't locked from the inside as it usually was . . . Pedrinho tried the lock—it was loose. With a little push the gate was open.

Pedrinho was already gathering *jabuticabas* from a tree trunk, choosing the largest and quickly filling his pockets for a fast getaway, when he heard a voice.

"So it's you! Just wait till Godmother sees."

* A round, black, smooth-skinned fruit, about the size of a cherry; it grows on the trunk and main branches of the *jabuticabeira* tree.

Confused, he stopped immediately and looked around —but saw no one.

"Here, silly."

Nazaré was in that very tree, leaning against a high branch, her feet in a fork, her dress wrapped tightly about her legs.

"How did you get up there?"

"I climbed."

"Did you? Well, I want to see you climb down."

"You won't because I won't let you. What an idea!"

That was enough to confuse him utterly. He only wanted to get away from there, but would that be impolite?

"Don't blush. Just turn your back while I come down," she offered, helping him out of his dilemma.

He quickly obeyed and even lowered his head as an additional guarantee. A twig snapped, *jabuticabas* rained on the ground soft with dried leaves and old kindling, and then Pedrinho felt Nazaré's soft breath on his ear. He turned his face toward her but she was already on the other side of the tree. He tried again but she moved quickly.

"You don't have to hide from me. I'm on my way," he muttered, frustrated.

"Where to?"

"None of your business."

"Well, nasty. Just because I didn't want you to watch me coming down there's no reason to be rude."

He felt his ears get hot and his face get prickly. Women

seemed to live just to exasperate men. What should he do? Swear? Run off? Better not do anything.

"Oh, silly. There's no reason to get red like that. I'm just teasing."

"Well, I don't like games like that," he said obstinately.

"What kind of games do you like?"

"None."

The reply escaped his lips before he could stop it, and now it was too late; he couldn't give a different answer. Because of that answer the courtship might end then and there if Nazaré didn't save it.

"Do you know something?" she asked, twisting a button on his jacket. "You're too serious. You act like a priest. Your blessing, Monsignor."

He pretended to be very indignant (he had to do something), and pushed her hand away roughly.

"Don't say that again."

She accepted the challenge and, leaning forward, her face almost touching his, repeated, "Padre! Padre! Padre Pedrinho!" He tried to catch her by the arm and she wriggled away, leading him on. A chase among the *jabuticabeiras* ensued, with Nazaré hiding behind a tree trunk, flitting to another, laughing, threatening; she concealed herself in a banana grove, Pedrinho found her—and then when he had her by the wrist, he had no idea what to do next.

"Well, did I catch you or not?"

"Only because I was getting tired. Let me go, you're hurting me."

He released her at once. Disappointed, she avenged herself:

"You're well-trained, aren't you?"

He grabbed her again, this time by the waist, with both hands. It was the first time he had ever been so close to a woman. Now what? How could he keep from ruining this moment?

Nazaré was watching him breathlessly, waiting. She must do nothing to drive him away. There must be no turning back now—it could mean total defeat for both of them.

It was such an intense moment that she experienced fear—of everything, of losing him—and because of this she put her arms around his waist, held him tightly and hid her face in his chest. Quietly, they remained that way, suffering, living, silent.

*Sabiás** sang in the *jabuticabeiras,* in the distance roosters and hens were carried away in raucous lovemaking. A horse whinnied on the other side of the river and shot off in a joyous gallop through pastures dyed with sunshine.

When Pedrinho calmed down enough to be able to notice the glorious smell of Nazaré's hair—not the smell of perfume or lotion or pomade, but the smell of pure hair; hair and skin and innocent sweat, the halo that accompanies every woman on the eve of love—he thrust his face into the softness of it, pushing through the hair instinctively to reach the warmth at the nape of her neck. She aided him with gentle, nestling movements, knowing that

* Brazilian mocking-thrushes.

his intuitions were right. Then came the embrace, all fury, rage, and haste; the urgent and careful kisses; haste again, shortened breath, near suffocation . . .

Where were they? In a banana grove, among bees and leaves and garden smells, under a festive sky. Nazaré took her arms away and asked Pedrinho to release her; he obeyed, half dazed. She straightened her dress, sighed deeply, and smoothed her hair, knowing as she did so that it would have to be done all over again.

They stayed there a long time, silent, clinging together, getting to know one another, until they heard Dona Bita calling Nazaré. Only then did Nazaré remember that she had come out to pick *jabuticabas* for her godmother, and the basket was still empty. Pedrinho helped her fill the basket, quickly and none too carefully. A last, fleeting kiss and Nazaré returned to the house. Pedrinho went out, closing the gate as slowly and gently as if it were a treasure chest, and was enveloped in a new and friendly world.

With shyness gone, discretion also disappeared. The two met anywhere, at any time, always with the intention of keeping it short. The intention was immediately forgotten. Surprised at the change in Pedrinho, Seu Quinel began to take note of his tardiness for a future lecture, in case the boy failed to improve. Relatives on one side and the other delivered warnings and advice. Dona Bita heard denunciations and broad hints all day long; she reached the stage where she dreaded meeting acquaintances or receiving callers. They greeted her, asked about her health, grumbled about the weather, coughed, and then poured out their unwelcome information.

"You know, Dona Bita, I saw your goddaughter over in Rosario Alley. She's looking very thin."

"Dona Bita, I know it isn't any of my business, but since I'm your friend . . ."

"I think you should take steps. Your goddaughter is getting herself talked about."

Sometimes Dona Bita felt like lashing out, asking them to leave the courting couple in peace, but she hadn't the nerve. She understood that these women, in their apparent malice, really meant well; perhaps Nazaré and Pedrinho actually were going too far. Could she be failing in her duty because of soft-heartedness or self-indulgence?

When she tried to censure her goddaughter, the girl's reply—so reasonable—put an end to the matter.

"It's a courtship, Godmother. We're not doing anything we shouldn't."

"Then why don't you court here at home and avoid all the talk?"

"They'd talk just the same. It would be even worse. They'd say you were 'aiding and abetting.'"

Dona Bita thought of this possibility and decided Nazaré was right. Courting is courting and always gives rise to talk. Anyone who listens is a fool.

Seu Quinel also suffered a certain amount of pressure at home, but he defended Pedrinho whenever he could. One day his wife, complaining that she could no longer walk through Rosario Alley because of the goings-on, insisted that he speak to the boy.

"But I can't, Santa. He's not my son, he's no concern of mine."

"No concern of yours? Isn't he your employee? Employers have rights, I'll have you know! Don't you pay him every month? Then you have the right to insist on his behaving properly."

"I can't, Santa. It wouldn't look right. I spoke to him about his tardiness, and he improved. But I can't interfere in matters of courtship."

"If you won't speak to him, I will. You know I mean it."

Quinel sighed and promised to see what he could do.

"Seeing what you can do is not enough. You should tell him to stop that shameful conduct. And don't try to fool me. I'll find out whether you said anything to him or not."

Quinel suffered through a whole day trying to find the courage to approach the subject. It was not that he was afraid Pedrinho would fly off the handle; Pedrinho was a very quiet boy, even shy. But he had scruples about meddling in the private life of an employee. In the evening, as Pedrinho was putting on his jacket to leave the store, Seu Quinel called out to him.

"Pedrinho, I'd like to ask you a favor. When you are out walking with Nazaré, please avoid Rosario Alley."

Pedrinho stared at him, uncomprehending, one arm stiff behind him, aimed at a sleeve.

"Rosario Alley? Why, Seu Quinel?"

"Just a whim of mine. As a favor."

Pedrinho finished putting on his jacket, pulled it down back and front, straightened his shirt inside his coat sleeve; he said nothing because he was trying to find some reason for the unusual request.

114

"Will you promise?"

"I promise, Seu Quinel."

"And another thing; don't tell anyone I asked you."

Pedrinho departed, more intrigued than ever. This court-ship affected everything. There seemed to be opposition on all sides, a new vexation daily. Nazaré was going through the same thing. Oh, if only they could run away somewhere where nobody could see them. But a place like that only existed in Paradise.

They started to meet on the paths on the other side of the river, frequented only by people from the outskirts collecting firewood, cane to build shacks with, or roots for medicines, and they paid no attention to them. Or there were small boys after birds, very busy at their nooses and snares and with no interest or time for spying on lovers.

Nazaré's relationship with her godmother was also be-coming difficult. Dona Bita thought she was being left alone too much; often when she needed Nazaré the girl was not at home and did not come home for a long time. At first Dona Bita didn't complain, but her long sighs communicated disapproval of the shape things were tak-ing. Then, having no one else to talk to, she began to confide in the cat, Fidalgo, a lazy mass of white fur and yellow eyes that spent its time sleeping on the furniture, usually where she had just put down her sewing. She be-gan by speaking to him only when she was alone, but she occasionally forgot herself and conversed with the cat in Nazaré's presence. Nazaré heard and understood but kept

115

quiet, not wanting to discuss the situation. Since in a house filled with sighs and recriminations nobody can be happy, the two of them grew further and further apart, each a prisoner of her own thoughts.

The first serious clash came when Dona Bita wanted Nazaré to stay home for the visit of some relatives.

"Ah, no, Godmother. I can't stand those people."

"What have they ever done to you?"

"Nothing. But the kids are such brats!"

"They are my nephews. It's just as if they were your cousins."

"Not mine. My cousins aren't as silly as that."

Dona Bita said nothing while she digested the insult. Nazaré was sorry immediately but decided that the unfortunate thing had been said, the damage could not be undone.

"Sometimes I think you are beginning to bear me a grudge," said the godmother, without raising her eyes from her sewing.

Nazaré denied it, out of compassion.

"What nonsense, Godmother. Why?"

"I don't know why. I've searched for a reason and I can't think of one, but I do think so sometimes."

"You shouldn't think that way."

"Who can control thoughts? I'm alone here, and thoughts come without my inviting them. I try to fight them and convince myself they're not true but, when the time comes to prove it, you yourself make me begin to wonder again."

"But I haven't said anything."

"It's not what you say, it's what you do."

Nazaré understood and kept still. Would she really have to break her date with Pedrinho? Dona Bita noticed her confusion and took advantage of it.

"All I ask is this one little thing, and you refuse me."

"But Godmother, I shouldn't have to stay because of your visitors. They're not coming to see me."

"You are a part of the family."

"Unfortunately."

Nazaré said it without thinking; when she realized what she had said, she was filled with shame.

Dona Bita dropped her sewing and gazed at Nazaré, silent and wounded. Finally she spoke.

"So this is the thanks I get. I'd rather not have any."

Nazaré tried to put her arms around her, but Dona Bita turned away, offended. So many years of dedication were repudiated with one word. The truth had come to light at last, the real truth, hidden by the requirements of gratitude but strong and quick to crop up in a moment's thoughtlessness.

"Godmother, I didn't mean to say it, please don't cry."

"How can I help it? Do you think I have no feelings? Do you think everyone has a hard heart?"

Even as she consoled her, Nazaré half suspected that the weeping was out of proportion to the hurt, and noticed that the more she said the more Dona Bita wept. Nazaré wanted to go on talking, soothing her (her age, her kindness, her lonely life), but something very strong inside her would not permit her to collaborate in what she considered a farce; so she just held Dona Bita tight and said nothing more. The weeping went on, puny, sob-punctuated, irrelevant. Eventually Dona Bita put her wrist to her face and wiped her eyes.

"Don't pay any attention to me, Za. I'm an old fool. You go off on your date."

All the tenderness that Nazaré had been holding back brimmed over in a flood of kisses and hugs no longer repelled.

"I'm an old fool," repeated Dona Bita, weeping and smiling at the same time. "Be patient with me."

NAZARÉ AND PEDRINHO were kissing in the shade of a bamboo thicket close to Cattle Spring when the men passed in their dilapidated carriage. There were two of them, one in front driving and the other sprawled on the back seat. The carriage passed them, went on a few yards, and stopped. The two strangers whispered to each other, and the one who was riding in the back leaned out and called arrogantly:

"You there. Come over here."

The lovers stood staring, uncomprehending. The man repeated:

"Come here."

Pedrinho looked at Nazaré and back at the men.

"Me?"

"Both of you."

118

Pedrinho hesitated, trying to think of a way to refuse without offending them.

"Go on," said Nazaré, giving him a little push.

Pedrinho went over, unwillingly. The man watched him calmly, waiting. When Pedrinho reached the carriage, the man spoke.

"You are Pedro Afonso."

Pedrinho nodded; he saw no reason to be friendly toward these men.

"And that's Nazaré."

Another mute confirmation. The man seemed to be waiting for some sign of surprise, or at least curiosity, at this show of knowledge; not getting one, he took back his smile and spoke with some severity.

"Don't you two think you've chosen the wrong place for this kind of activity?"

"No, I don't," Pedrinho replied, seething with rage at this impertinence.

"Well, it is. Isn't it, Osorio?"

The other agreed, adding:

"It's dangerous. Bamboos breed snakes."

"See?" asked the man behind. "Snakes. Aren't you scared, girl?"

"Snakes!" cried Nazaré, alarmed.

"Why don't you two come and court in the compound? It's perfect. There are benches and hammocks, you can do what you like; and there's nobody to bother you."

Pedrinho had not yet adjusted to the new situation and the man was already suggesting:

"Get in. The horse can take it, can't he, Osorio?"

"He's got to. He has no choice."

"Get the girl. I'll go in front," said the other, jumping out of the carriage and, in his hurry, letting his hat fall. Pedrinho lifted his knee to try and catch it, but it rolled down his leg and under the carriage. "Leave it," ordered the man, "when we start moving I'll reach down and grab it," as if Pedrinho were making a particular effort to retrieve it, which he was not.

Pedrinho made a sign to Nazaré and she came quickly, as if she had been waiting for his gesture.

"Do you want to come?"

"Yes! Come on! How d'you get into this thing?"

The man helped her get in, lifting her unceremoniously by the waist. As the carriage started up the man retrieved his hat, beat the dust off it, ran and leaped to the front seat, squeezing himself in next to the other one.

"You two haven't been there yet," he said, after he was settled. "You're going to like it. 'Specially her."

The lovers did not reply; it was not a question but an announcement, even a promise.

The carriage rolled over ground never intended for traffic. The crossbar groaned, the bumps caused jolts and jerks and jarring, the horses moaned and snorted under their burden, until eventually they reached town. As they crossed the square, people turned and craned their necks to see who was inside and, when they recognized the passengers, they looked again to make sure they were seeing right; some still could not believe it and chased the vehicle, not wanting to be left in doubt.

"Well, what about that! Did you see?"

"Do you think they've been kidnapped?"

"No, they didn't look like it. They even looked happy."

"But the ones in front looked grim."

"Well, they're like that."

The carriage proceeded alongside the square, attracting disbelieving stares. Nobody could explain it—Nazaré and Pedrinho going by in the compound's carriage, as happy as children getting a lift in a truck. It caused quite a flutter among the young men, all attired in their Sunday best, shoes highly polished, hair continually tended in case a lock got out of line, jackets buttoned, unbuttoned, buttoned again, in order to be seen in all their elegance, trouser creases constantly defended (any boy whose clothing misbehaved, or who lost face for not being fashionable, had to wait a full week to redeem himself).

When the carriage was out of sight, conversation veered toward Pedrinho's courtship. Who would have thought that quiet, shy boy, always pointed out as an example, would end up with his shirttail showing, defying the whole town with his determined courting?

"Well, he's no stick-in-the-mud now."

"He's learned not to ask the bishop's by-your-leave."

"He had a good teacher."

The girls passed by, walking arm in arm in the opposite direction, whispering, giggling, and casting glances; they went in and out of the houses, always giggling and whispering. The boys watched them, remembered the girls had fathers or older brothers, and envied Pedrinho his good fortune.

When she heard that Nazaré and Pedrinho had been seen in the compound's carriage, Dona Bita was troubled. She had nothing personal against the men. She even enjoyed being greeted by them when she was at the window (they took their hats off completely, hardly anyone did that in Manirema), but outsiders—and rather strange ones at that, with a habit of speaking in an undertone among themselves, of stopping and pointing to one thing and another, as if measuring, evaluating, taking note—well, one cannot be too careful with outsiders.

Dona Bita went to the back window, made binoculars of her hands, and watched the road. The carelessness of those two, getting mixed up with strangers when there were so many places to go! Why not go up to Santa Barbara Church on top of the hill? That was where courting couples used to go, not alone, of course, but with the girl's family, taking along cookies, fruit brandy, the makings of coffee. The boys brought a guitar, a flute, a ukelele, and sang and played until night fell, only coming down when the moon was high. Nowadays nobody wants to learn to play a musical instrument, they either have no time or they think it silly. With a great deal of persuasion they might learn to play the guitar and then go and strum it in bars frequented by women of low repute. Manirema had changed a great deal. It was said to be the same all over, the whole world had changed, but Manirema seemed to have changed more . . .

Dona Bita got tired of watching; she did not catch sight of the carriage. It was no use staying at the window; the compound could not be seen from there, only the woods and the smoke from their cooking fires. Those people must eat huge amounts. The stoves in the compound never stopped smoking, and they all looked fat and sleek. But the things they ate! Tree fungus, bamboo shoots, banana navels, wormy cheese, the wormier the better (this was hard to believe, but if it was a lie, then Geminiano was a liar). How can you possibly trust people who eat such odd food? The sad thing was that some folks in Manirema were making an effort to adopt those very foods; men obliged their wives to cook bamboo shoots, ate them with feigned enjoyment, and then asked for more. But the children spat them out and left their plates full.

Now that one thought of it, only the children of Manirema were refusing the new ideas copied from the men in the compound. The grown-ups were full of expedients, whether from hope of advantages to be gained or just plain fear. People like Apolinario were rare, and remained isolated. Even their families gave them softening advice, based on better-careful-now-than-sorry-later, think-it-over, hold-a-candle-to-the-devil schools of thought. And now Nazaré was with them, might even catch their habit of eating wormy cheese; that is where they would really have a falling-out. No one in her house had better even consider eating wormy cheese!

Having reached that decision, Dona Bita calmed down. She would get dressed, comb her hair, and go to the window to await her visitors.

THE TIME
OF THE OXEN

F OR SOME DAYS oxen had been appearing here and
there, on the slopes of the hills, on the plains, at the
edge of the roads, peaceful and unconcerned. The brands
they carried revealed nothing, being either unknown in
that region or so faint they were hard to decipher. They
must be runaway cattle, strayed from their herds; any day
now the owners would come to fetch them, or they would
disappear by themselves just as they had come —with no
warning or fuss.

That was what everyone thought, but it was not what
happened. Instead of going away, the oxen kept coming
in greater and greater numbers. They took over all the
roads leading to the town. They crossed the river on one
side, the brook on the other, always converging on the
town. In no time at all there they were, licking at the
walls of the outlying houses, fat, tame, and filthy. They
crowded through the streets and alleys, spilling over into
the square. The invasion was quick and without incident,
and when the people realized what was happening it was
too late to do anything about it. Oxen lay in pathways,
obstructing passages and terrifying the women; the en-
trances to the square were choked with animals and more
were coming, as if called by a horn that was audible only

to them. Oxen unable to squeeze into the square took over the nearby streets, the alleys, and the empty lots. Anyone opening a window to investigate the weather got a full dose of bull's breath in the face. People absentmindedly entering a thicket got the fright of their lives when the bulls dashed out, trampling plants and trailing branches from their horns. Hurrying around a corner, people fell unseeingly onto the horns of an ox.

All day and night more oxen kept coming, trampling everything in their path. They knocked down the shanties of the poor, invaded the streets of the rich, crushed against each other, heads up to avoid locking horns. They did not even have the space to lift up their tails to defecate; the filth slid down their legs, defiling everything.

The townspeople could no longer leave their houses. The oxen served the same purpose as bars on the doors, and would not let anyone pass; they could not, there was no room for them to move. Once a window was opened, it was impossible to close it, nothing was strong enough to push back that mass of horns, heads, and necks that now took up every inch of space.

Often fighting broke out, and the shocks reverberated far and wide; distant walls fell down and new clashes began until the shoving, butting, and bumping forced the animals into some temporary resolution. An ox that lost its footing in a collision and went down on its knees was unable to rise; the others trampled it until it died. One less made for a little more room, but only until a surge from elsewhere again renewed the pressure.

On the slopes the weaker oxen dropped, exhausted with the effort of remaining upright against the avalanche pressing down from above. They fell and rolled against the legs of the other animals, bringing them down too, until, stopped by some wall, gully, or tree, they lay crushed and broken and moaning. Garden walls and fences that had held up well in the first few hours now sagged and caved in with the mounting pressure and, as water when a dam breaks, the bulls spilled out, tumbling, leaping, butting, ruining the planting and terrifying pigs and chickens.

Even inside their houses the townspeople could not relax. Those who had not taken the precaution of closing the windows at the very beginning were now obliged to do everything under the gaze of two or three pairs of bovine eyes. Sometimes they even had to force a horn aside in order to open a drawer or a cupboard.

If it had not been for the cleverness of the small boys who invented a means of walking on the backs of the oxen, the families would have been in a state of siege inside their homes, with no means of communicating with friends or relatives. Barefoot and armed with a pole that had a quilted pad tied to one end of it, the boys climbed on the window sills and, using the pole as a brace, traveled over the top of the animals carrying messages back and forth, and even challenging each other to races. Occasionally a small boy missed his footing, or the ox moved as he stepped onto it, and he was plunged down into the mire. Some boys were able to crawl among the maze of hooves,

129

filthying themselves in the dung, getting soaked in the pools of urine, bloodying hands and knees on the sharp gravel, until they reached the shelter of a ditch or the steps of a doorway. But many of them got turned around and lost their way; those who screamed and frightened the oxen ended up crushed by the beasts.

No one was able to sleep that night, despairing at the constant bellowing of the animals and the fear of a stampede. The walls would never withstand the pressure of a stampede; even the most solid houses would cave in, and bracing would do no good—the props would push out the walls and the roof would collapse.

During the long hours filled with oppressive lowing, the townspeople whiled away the time sitting on their porches, sipping herb drinks, and wondering what they had done to deserve such punishment. The men smoked incessantly, the women murmured every prayer they knew for times of affliction. Occasionally a woman would get up quickly and run to the kitchen to attend a crying child bedded down in the oven, the only place in the house that could offer some measure of safety. The most absurd defense plans were made—such as eliminating the oxen by wholesale poisoning of the grass or the water—but quickly abandoned for lack of means to implement them.

The more serious citizens tried to soothe the others, claiming that although the present was dark, all would soon be well; the right conditions did not exist for so many cattle to stay any length of time. They needed pasture and a lot of water and one of these days they would be forced to go back to the meadows they came from, unable to find what they needed in the town. All Manirema would have to do was wait and trust. If the walls held up and provisions held out, soon they would all be out in the streets celebrating the town's liberation. The place for an ox is either field or corral. Who knew, perhaps they would disappear tomorrow.

But at daybreak the oxen were still there, implanted, motionless, a monstrous obstacle. The optimists, who had hoped ingenuously to open their windows in the morning and find the landscape unencumbered, found themselves faced instead with an expanse of rumps steaming with dew, forming a sort of awning over the ground, as rolling as the terrain it covered and stretching as far as the eye could see. What could they be doing there, and how long could they be expected to stay? Where did they belong, who could be their master?

As the sun came up, the dew began to dry and the hides regained their shine. The cattle wakened out of the torpor of the night and started the same pushing and pressing, lowing and bellowing. The small boys, playing their new game of leap-the-ox, passed by, giving out the news.

"There's bulls even in the church. They've chewed up the altar cloths and knocked over the candlesticks."

"The cemetery is smothered in oxen."

"The dam at the sugar mill is all clogged up with drowned bulls."

"The river's filled with them; they're even standing on top of each other."

131

"The bridge is sagging with the weight of them. It'll cave in any minute now."

"You know those locust trees in the Golden Grotto? There are even bulls in the branches. Sometimes one falls out and smashes on the rocks below."

"All the roads are taken over. Nobody can get by."

"On Straw Street there isn't a single shanty left standing."

Families could no longer go into their backyards; they had to relieve themselves in old pots, newspapers, and odd boxes, and then keep it all in a corner in the hope of better days. Water was getting scarce; the small boys were unable to refill the jars and tins because there was no way to reach the fountain; they hardly knew where it was any more. Coffee couldn't be made, nor dishes washed; what water remained was hoarded for drinking and cooking.

The evening of the second day, when the oxen still stood there unmoving, Father Prudente began to receive appeals to do something, anything, to rid the town of the cattle —to offer prayers, say litanies, things of that nature. Boys arrived constantly, jumped from the back of an ox to his window, from the window into the room, asked his blessing, delivered the message, and stood leaning on their poles as they waited for an answer. The good father would scratch his head, stare at the field of horns spread out before him, and promise to think about it. Finally he closed the windows and stared instead at his stamp collection.

132

But now the requests came from inside the house, José Balduino and the cook, Maria Menina, taking turns.

"Father, go and bless those oxen. There's barely a drop of water at the bottom of the jar," the cook begged.

"We'll see, we'll see. Afterward," soothed the padre, leafing through the pages of his stamp album.

"Father, while those animals are here, people could die without confessing themselves," reminded José Balduino.

"It's God's will, Balduino. It's an act of God."

"But it won't hurt you to bless them. The people are asking for it."

"It's dangerous, Balduino. They might take fright at the vestments. Think of the consequences."

At times encouraging rumors ran riot, and the towns-people gained heart.

"They seem to be moving up by the cemetery. There's already lots of empty spaces on the football field."

"People up at Agua Limpa are able to leave their houses. The oxen have gone from there."

Everyone then waited for his own street to unclog; they would give it a few minutes, run to the window, and come back discouraged. The oxen were still there, as tightly pressed together as raisins in a box.

And the stories were soon denied. The boys ran in all directions inspecting, and they always returned to say the same thing: even if the oxen wanted to go away, there was no way for them to move. The roads were filled as far as the eye could see. It looked as though one could go all the way to Quintacruz, Paiol do Meio, Salvosseja, or

133

Jasminópolis treading on ox backs. The whole world belonged to the oxen. There was no room for any other beast; pity the poor armadillo and cavy, the partridge and the crested sariema, even the ants, or the fish unable to swim in the obstructed rivers.

But as they say: one man's poison is another man's meat—the ticks never had it so good! They lived the life of Riley, clinging to the skins of the oxen, gorging contentedly, changing in no time from little brown confetti to pot-bellied blue gourds. (Unfortunately for them, the good life lasted but a short time; as soon as they fattened they were pried off to help fill the stomach of some other ravening animal; the only lucky ones were those fastened to the beasts' underbellies.)

The postmaster, taking advantage of the goodwill of the young boys, organized a messenger service for the town. The boys were separated into two teams, one to gather messages at the windows and take them to the post office, and the other to deliver them to their destinations; small packages could also be picked up and delivered. That way, someone with a little water to spare could share a bottle or a cupful with whoever had none or who needed an extra amount to make tea for a sick person.

When the boys arrived home at night they had barely enough strength to lean their poles in a corner before they dropped from exhaustion. Their mothers came running with a cookie, a baked potato, brown-sugar scrapings, took one look at their sleeping sons, and lacked the courage to wake them. Instead, they left the food nearby, sometimes even on the floor, kissed the small, worn face, and went back to suffer out the rest of the night beside their husbands.

Living like prisoners in their own homes, the people stared at their clothes on the hangers, their shoes under the beds, and sighed, wondering if the day would ever come when they would wear them again.

The news was not good. Dismal reports came from every direction. No matter how far the boys went on their inspection tours, they saw nothing to suggest that the mass was thinning out. People began to feel that the very air was getting scarce inside the houses.

Whenever the boys stopped off at their homes for a moment, to rest or eat, they would tell of what they had seen and heard. On Stone Street a man had gone berserk and run out of his house to rain blows on the cattle; he was crushed to death; no one could help him. On Roqueiras Street another man tried to walk on the cattle's backs as the boys did; at his first leap, he slipped and drowned. Seu Alipio's vineyard was gone. In Big Quarry Alley some bulls, attracted by the smell of urine on the diaper of a child sleeping in its cradle under the window, ate all the cloth in the cradle and then skinned the child alive with their rasping tongues.

There was general despair. Everyone realized that Manirema was doomed and could only be saved by a miracle. When Joaquim Rufino, the only prisoner in the jail, saw the trouble the boys were taking to keep him supplied with food and water, he took up his guitar, sat on the sill

135

of his barred window, and made up a song for the bulls. The boys who heard it liked it, but were unable to repeat it properly at home. If Joaquim did not make a copy it would be lost. But why trouble to write verses down on paper, when everything was coming to an end? The jail, too, with its thick walls and bars of pepper-tree wood reinforced with iron, would disappear; and the paper would vanish with it. Manirema was doomed.

QUITE EARLY one rain-threatened morning, Pedrinho Alfonso leaped from the back of an ox through Dona Bita's window into her parlor. He stood there leaning against the window sill, his face hidden in his arms, trembling like a leaf. When Dona Bita happened into the room she was so alarmed she could not move or use her voice. A strange man in the house, and on such a day! But she reminded herself that she was alone, shouting for help would be useless, and there was nowhere to hide. She tried to regain her calm, looked again, and saw that it was Pedrinho.

"May our good Lady help me, son! What a fright you gave me! Are you ill? How did you get here?"

"No, I'm not ill, Godmother. I'm just tired."

"Where did you come from?"

"From there."

"And Nazaré? What happened to her?"

He started to speak, but bit his lips and shrugged instead.

"Did you leave my girl there? Alone with those men? Oh, Pedrinho, how could you?"

136

"She jilted me. I haven't seen Nazaré since Sunday. I ran away."

"And her?"

"She's there with them."

Dona Bita grabbed his arms, shook him hard, and insisted:

"Pedrinho, tell me the truth. What did you do to my girl?"

Pedrinho lowered his head and corrected her in a small voice that trembled with fury:

"Nothing. They were the ones."

"What did they do?"

"They did . . . you know what they did."

"Pedrinho, tell me the truth or I'll—"

They looked out at the square taken over by the bulls and both realized the idle nature of any threat. Her tone turned to pleading.

"I have to know, Pedrinho. What happened to her?"

"They took her from me and brought her inside. I resisted. A bunch of them held me. I shouted and cursed and bit them. They tied me up. She helped. Nazaré helped them! They stuffed my mouth with rags. She helped. They threw me into a hole in the back. Look at these rope burns. They gave me food in a clay bowl on the ground. I had to put my face in it to eat, like a dog. She would stay nearby, watching me; sometimes she'd push the bowl away with her foot just to see me drag myself on the earth. At daybreak today I got my hands loose, so I untied the ropes and escaped."

Dona Bita raised her hand to her brow and shook her head slowly.

"Nazaré did that? My Nazaré did a thing like that? You're not making it up?"

"No, I'm not, Godmother. You should see what she is like now. She's a different person."

"She didn't scream? She wasn't afraid of the men?"

"Afraid? She was afraid of nothing! When one of them got the idea of tying me up and everything, you should have seen how pleased she was. She was jumping around and rubbing her hands with glee. She even encouraged the others."

Dona Bita covered her mouth with her hand and stood staring at the floor. Little by little her face got hard, her eyes narrowed, her mouth tightened. Eventually she spoke, fierce with hatred:

"I knew it! I knew that girl was going to disappoint me. Nazaré never was any good. From the time she was small she showed what she was. I was the one who closed my eyes. I pretended she was a loving, grateful girl because that was what I needed for company. Many people came to warn me, but when I heard them criticize her I became even more stubborn. I knew they could see through what I said, but I was not going to give them my arm to twist. All those nights I spent praying for a miracle, asking God to make her the girl I pretended she was—I was stupid and now I'm paying for it. But I was getting old, with no time left to start over. I thought it would be easier to pretend she was turning out like I wanted her to . . . I also thought that I might die before . . . before I was terribly disappointed in her."

Dona Bita dried her tears (there were not very many) and stared at the floor as though she thought a solution to the crisis could be found in those old, warped, creaking boards, in a strange code that only she could decipher.

Pedrinho was wandering through tangled thoughts: a dense thicket, no light, ox legs, navels, dewlaps, a bog of dung and urine, horns, lowing; an evil world.

"Pedrinho . . . You have no father or mother. Stay and live with me. You will be like my son."

Dona Bita's words penetrated slowly, echoing in his mind. He had endured the greatest difficulties getting back to the town, and several times had thought he would never reach the square. Live there how long? One day? Two? A week, if that much? How could anyone think of the future, or make any plans? Manirema's future was death and decay in the filth, the carnage of oxen covering everything, the sun drying it, rain watering it, swamps, beetles, ants, termites, worms, grass growing from seeds discharged in the manure, no one alive to cut it and re-place it and look after it, the jungle taking over, trees growing inside the houses, pushing up the roofs, forcing the walls out, snakes making nests in the stoves, lizards sleeping in the cracks, vines winding themselves around everything, Manirema a wasteland. But what would be the use of saying all this to Dona Bita?

"Thank you, Godmother. I'll stay here with you."

She put her arms around him and then had a good look

139

at the boy, discovering immediately that something must be done about his hair, his clothes, his face.

"You'll have to change those clothes. Your shirt is filthy. And look at your trousers, what a mess! You look as if you'd been sleeping on the ground." Suddenly remembering what he had just told her, his face thrust in a bowl like a dog's, she went on hastily: "There's not even enough water to wash your face, but I'll go and see about a towel so you can wipe yourself more or less clean."

While Dona Bita was getting the towel, Pedrinho looked at himself in the big parlor mirror and almost took fright at the image. What he saw was a boy who would never become a man, who would not be a husband or a father to anyone, would never have white hair, or suffer from rheumatism. And would that be so bad, after all?

Dona Bita returned with a damp towel and began to wipe his face, his ears inside and out, hands, arms, neck, stopping occasionally to search for a clean spot on the towel.

"You can have Nazaré's room. Later I'll change things around a bit, take off all those frills and throw them out."

He was about to ask "Later than what?" but thought it better not to spoil the old woman's delusion, even if she was just trying to fool herself, it did not cost him anything to be silent.

"Heavens! What kind of a head have I got?" she exclaimed suddenly. "I haven't offered you a thing to eat. Well, there's only brown-sugar scrapings and manioc flour. Will that do?"

He said he was not hungry, but she paid no heed and brought him a plate of flour and scrapings.

"I sprinkled it a little on top so that it wouldn't be too dry. The water's about finished."

He sat on the couch with the plate in his lap, took a spoonful, and gazed out the window while the mixture dissolved in his mouth. Why eat if in a few days' time there would be nothing left to eat?

Dona Bita put her hand on his shoulder.

"Don't think about her any more, Pedrinho. She isn't worth the bother. For me she is already dead."

Instead of explaining, he handed her the plate.

"I really don't want it, Godmother. I'll eat it later."

"Then you lie down a bit and rest. Lie down right there. I'll bring you a pillow."

He spent the remainder of the day in anguish and dread. Often he awakened in terror, reliving in horrible dreams the torments he so recently suffered—perverse men committing acts of insanity, oxen with nightmarish faces destroying the whole world in wild rampage, bellowing like mocking laughter. He took deep breaths and looked at the furniture in the parlor, the photographs and prints on the wall; he had to touch the cane on the back of the settee to convince himself that he was safe. His eyes closed and he drifted back into sleep, only to waken again, shaken by new terrors.

The small boys no longer came by on courier missions; they were too weak. The town was slowly dying. The church clock had stopped striking. The stone weight that turned the rope's mechanism was probably lying on the floor of the tower cellar. Now no one would climb the stairs to turn the handle that lifted the stone. It would be a wasted effort; soon there would be no more hours to record. And it was fitting that the clock should be silent, as its regular striking would be an unwelcome reminder, another reason for despair.

Anyone still disposed to go to the window and gaze at the sky saw the vultures flying in high, scattered circles, wheeling lazily and patiently. They had received the call and the ritual had begun. As the days advanced they would come lower, the circles closer together, the wheeling becoming faster and faster until the final frenzy before possession.

The mixed odors of wet horns, hides, and urine, barely noticed during the first days, now tainted the air, nauseating everyone. Headaches, dizziness, and vomiting were commonplace, especially among the children. Anything that was eaten or drunk, even whisky, had that sour smell the townspeople had begun to associate with the odor of death. To disguise it they burned orange peels, ginger grass, tobacco, anything they could find at home or pick in the garden by leaning out the kitchen window.

Weakened by hunger and frequent vomiting, the people spent most of their time lying in silence, staring at the roof tiles and walls, lacking even the energy to think. The chairs around the tables, cupboards, brooms behind the doors, pictures of saints on the walls, water jars in the corners, all seemed useless leftovers of a distant and irrecoverable way of life. A hat that fell off a hook stayed on the floor, for the effort of picking it up would have been greater than its usefulness. Despairing sighs were heard from all sides, but no one could feel compassion; another man's sighs were nothing compared to one's own intimate suffering. They had become no more than commentaries on the general hopelessness. Manirema was at death's door, and nothing less than a miracle would save it.

NIGHT FELL. Hardly anyone lit lamps; there were few houses with anything left to light. And with everlasting night so near, lamps and candles would make little difference. In the resigned and spectral town only the wailing of the children and the whistling of the nighthawks penetrated the arrogant lowing. Nobody paid any further attention to what was happening outside. The oxen were obviously not leaving; the need was for sleep, forgetfulness, preparation. The remainder of life had to be lived inside oneself, the gates to the outside were virtually closed. That was why few people noticed the first signs, and even those who did attached no importance to them.

First it was a restlessness among the oxen, a movement of rumps and dewlaps, a scraping of hooves on the ground; then the intermingled lowing, calling, warning. Those who awoke at the unusual sounds dared not hope for more than to see the same sight when morning came: the oxen rooted there, stubborn, permanent, as they had been for days, for months, for centuries, perhaps; suffocating the town, separating friends. People forgot the color of the earth, the contours of the land, became confused about distances and routes, and wondered what a town would be like without bulls.

The ones who heard the early signals turned over and went back to sleep. Sleeping, at least, was one act that could be indulged in despite the oxen. But near daybreak the silence was like an explosion. Where was the bellowing, the snorting, the pounding in the mud, the scraping of horns, and where—above all—was that massive presence? It felt like the unexpected silence running water makes when it ceases in the middle of the night. It is an illusory silence because water does not dry up suddenly, it cannot stop or turn back; it is a quirk of nature or the air or the night—never a reason for alarm.

But the silence continued and, even inside the houses, in the dimness of bedrooms, the air was light, clean, free. Forgotten far-off noises—the howl of dogs, the shrill of crickets, the fall of ripe fruit in backyards, all the sounds that make up a normal night—were heard clearly, no longer muffled by a mass of skin and fur, muscle and bone, horns and lowing.

And, suddenly, the discovery! People ran to their windows, still apprehensive but beginning to hope. The shock, the disbelief, the joy! Open sky, empty streets, moonlight purifying the quagmire of urine and dung. Was it possible? People calling others, shaking one another, dragging others to see, all the windows opening, clear streets and emptiness in every direction. People laughing, jumping for joy, hugging and dancing in the ooze, dressing hastily and dashing outside, thumping on their neighbors' doors, shouting, shooting firearms. People appearing at windows, rubbing their eyes in disbelief, wanting to know what had happened and who did it. People singing in the streets, getting stuck in the mire, boots and all; groups rushing here and there, inspecting, recognizing, touching; small boys running to the fountain with buckets and jars, standing under the spigot with all their clothes on, splashing each other and finding it uproariously funny in spite of the early-morning chill. People hurrying to the stores, buying food for quick suppers, stoves being lit in the kitchens, firecrackers bursting all around, a band appearing from nowhere, more instruments constantly swelling its ranks; Joaquim Rufino yelling like a madman behind his bars, matching every hurrah with a curse, the judge taking pity and setting him free for the celebration (it might even be considered cause for amnesty; a petition would be entered the following day).

At times the moon was hidden by a dark mass of clouds, but nothing diminished the enthusiasm. Children built a bonfire at the door of the church, grown-ups gathered around it to bask in the warmth, bottles appeared in many a hand, and even the children were seen to sample them, but no one fussed—that night belonged to everyone; it had been hard earned. The dogs, shut inside the houses for so long or tied so as not to frighten the bulls, now came out to celebrate the liberation: they leaped up on their masters, mounted each other, growled and bit one another in play, ran between people's legs, and were not shouted at or smacked. People realized that dogs also had a right to be happy.

Someone arrived with a side of dried beef, another with a string of sausages. The children went off to find wood for spits. In the square itself there were a lot of bamboo canes scattered around (the difficulty was finding them in the ooze), and in no time at all the meat and sausage were sizzling in the flames. Attracted by the smell, the dogs stopped their nonsense and came to kibitz at the supper. People who lacked a knife or penknife ate with their hands. The dogs snapped up the pieces that fell off the improvised spits, swallowed them in one gulp, and waited for more, sitting attentively on their tails.

Heavy with sleep, the children started for home; some of the men also pleaded tiredness and excused themselves until the morning. When the bonfire eventually died down for lack of fuel, many had already left. The few that stayed, squatting around the dying fire, stared at the whitened embers, yawned and meditated. The time was not yet ripe for speech or the exchange of ideas. Tomorrow was on its way and people's unease was returning. Well or badly, the past had been overcome. Even terror, borne heaven knows how, had been conquered. But the evils yet unknown, the labor of making a clean start of their lives . . . would they really have learned something from this lesson?

An ember slipped, fell, broke into pieces, scattering sparks in every direction. A man rose, stretched, yawned, drew himself up on the tips of his toes.

"Well, folks, I'll be leaving."

146

"I'm going, too."

"Me, too," answered the others, rising and stretching, their joints cracking.

It occurred to one of them to pay homage to the remains of the bonfire by urinating on the dying embers. The others thought the idea a good one and did likewise, mostly to hear the urine hiss in the hot ashes. Then each one shoved his hands deep into his pockets, hunched his shoulders to protect his neck from the cold, and started homeward.

IT WAS RAINING the next day, gently, as if the rain were coming through a fine sieve. Gray mist covered the hills and the river, giving the landscape the look of a newborn world, a just-licked calf still glistening from its mother's tongue. Seated near the stove in smoky kitchens, the townspeople drank coffee and listened to the cries of the *sabiás* in the *jabuticabeira* trees. Nobody complained about the weather; the rain was a pretext to spend the day inside resting and taking stock.

Dona Bita was in the kitchen frying salt bacon that Pedrinho had gone to buy at Amancio Mendes' store, using an old women's umbrella (fortunately there had been no one there to make fun of him). When Dona Bita turned to reach for the little kettle where she kept the fat, she got the kind of shock that leaves one paralyzed, with the mouth open and the heart stopped. There stood Nazaré, soaking wet, numb with cold, wearing a cheap cotton handkerchief on her head, sneezing and coughing. She entered gropingly, hesitating, with so little assurance that she

147

could stay that she did not even remove her kerchief. Seeing her goddaughter standing there alone, water dripping
from her hair and clothes, feet thrust into slippers far too
big for them (a man's slippers, perhaps), Dona Bita
melted.

"Where in heaven is your sense, girl!" she said at last.
"Just look at those clothes! Soaking wet! Even your hair!
You'll get sick! Go change that dress and dry your hair.
Soak your feet in hot water and put on some socks. I'll heat
the water." To avoid explanations, she made herself busy
stoking the fire, adding water to the kettle, searching for
cinnamon in the cupboard to make a tonic.

"Godmother . . . I've come to stay," murmured Nazaré,
fearful that Dona Bita had misunderstood her reason for
being there.

But what Dona Bita did not understand was her state-
ment. She stopped, puzzled, the little bundle of cinnamon
sticks in her hand.

"To stay . . . ?"

"If you want me. If you'll let me."

"Goodness, girl! What a silly idea! Isn't this your home?
Where else would you go?"

"I don't know . . . I . . . forgive me, Godmother."
She began to sob as she reached for Dona Bita's hand
to kiss.

"This is no time for that," Dona Bita said roughly. "Go
and change those clothes at once. I don't want you to be
sick. And don't come out of that room. I'll bring in the
foot bath and the tea."

She was at the stove again when she remembered, and went to tell Nazaré:

"Tonight you're sleeping with me. Your room is taken."

Nazaré was too tired and defeated to ask questions. She wanted only to be accepted again, and that seemed to be settled. She went into Dona Bita's room and began to undress.

WITH THE RAIN Amancio Mendes did not expect too many customers, but he opened the store anyway and lounged against the counter, staring out at the alley. What bothered him most was that the manure made walking particularly difficult in the alley. In the streets the people managed somehow not to step all the way into the ooze. They used a stone here, a brick there, a tuft of weeds; but in the alley everything was covered over. How long was the sun going to take to harden all that muck after the rain, a piddly little one, nowhere near strong enough to wash away all that bull shit? And even when the sun did dry it, the fine dust, ground to a powder by animals' hooves and carried on the wind, would be around for a long time, a bitter reminder of the days just past. With that dust insinuating itself into everything, Manirema would have a hard time getting back to what it had been, if it ever could.

Manuel Florencio appeared in the doorway, removed the high wooden shoes made specially for the emergency, and entered the store barefoot. Amancio was so glad to see him that he jumped up and rushed to greet his friend.

"*Compadre! Compadre!* Well, now!"

149

Manuel seated himself on a sack of corn and lifted first one leg and then the other to roll down his trouser cuffs; there was no need to look like a backwoodsman.

"Well, *compadre*. Piddly little rain, isn't it?" said Amancio.

Manuel removed his hat, shook it and placed it on the floor, crown down so the water could drain off.

"It doesn't bother me. My work is indoors."

"Are you started up again?"

"I did a little planing to keep my hand in." He turned his head toward the door. "Some mud there, eh? It's going to take a long time for it to dry up. It must be more than a hand deep."

Amancio looked, too, not at the mud in the alley but above it, at all that lay ahead and beyond.

"The drying is nothing. The worst part is the dust. We're going to have that in our gullets for a long time, maybe for the rest of our lives."

"It will be good for the gardens," replied Manuel, always with an eye to the good side of things.

About midday the sky began to clear in parts and the sun showed itself, dimly and cautiously. People looked upward and felt less oppressed; the rifts in the mist seemed to help them breathe more freely. They began to venture out without the encumbrance of an umbrella; knots of people here and there tried to hold conversations, but most were unable to tear their attention away from the mud. The green rivulets forming in the pasty manure as the liquid tried to drain away or find a way out were an irresistible attraction. Some even helped with a stick, poking channels in the mire with the concentration they might give to performing an important task. Others gave their opinions on the pattern; still others participated only mentally, approving or disapproving without opening their mouths; the universal concern was with liberating the liquid from its muddy prison.

They were busy at this enterprise when Geminiano came by on his wagon, traveling very slowly because of his load, a high-piled mound of household trappings, including a mattress swaying precariously on one corner. Poor old Serrote strained to pull the weight and was forced to lift his hooves high, as if he were trotting, to free them of the slime. But Geminiano was whistling and brazenly greeting everyone right and left. People replied with some reserve, or did not reply at all; Geminiano's recent behavior was still too fresh in their minds.

At the dovecote corner, where a large crowd had gathered on the steps, he stopped on the pretext of having to rearrange his load. He got down, fussed with it here and there, pushed, pulled, thumped; eventually he gave up, looking satisfied in spite of having changed nothing, wiped his brow, and tried to start a conversation.

"Good thing the weather broke, eh?" He addressed the whole group, a precaution against a rebuff.

"Yes, indeed," replied one of the more polite.

"Sour kind of mud. Will take a long time to dry," Geminiano continued, encouraged by the first reply.

This time no one said anything. Geminiano drew in his

151

breath, let it out from puffed-up cheeks, making more noise than necessary.

"There's lots of good stuff in the compound. It's there for the taking," he offered, trying to please.

Nobody understood immediately; they all looked at him curiously. Having attracted their interest, he added:

"The men have gone."

"No!"

"Where?"

"Why?"

"When did they go?"

Geminiano let the questions pile up and gave a single answer.

"They flew the coop at daybreak."

"But why?"

"I think they were scared. They seemed kind of scared."

"Scared of what?"

"I don't know. Of everything. Of us. I mean, of all of you."

The people stared at each other incredulously. Could it be true? Was it possible? Or was Geminiano making it up?

"I don't believe it. He's talking through his hat. They told him to say it," warned a voice in the crowd.

"I swear to God. May I be blinded if it's not the truth." To prove it, he showed them the loaded wagon. "I took everything I wanted. It'll pay them back for what they owe me, the bunch of cheats."

The others exchanged ironic looks. Geminiano noticed and defended himself:

152

"Cheats! They never paid what they agreed, never. If it hadn't been for my wife killing herself over the stove and the sewing machine, we'd have gone hungry."

"Then why didn't you stop?"

"Because I know what's good for me. Ask Amancio why he didn't tell them off. Just ask him."

Amancio was approaching cautiously, picking his way through the slime. He did not hear the conversation, and nobody asked him anything. He got up on the sidewalk where the others were and scraped the soles of his ankle boots on the paving stones. Then he saw the loaded wagon.

"Moving, Gemi?"

"Moving back home, thank God."

"He says the men went away," someone reported.

"Did they? At last." Amancio said it as if he had been expecting the news. "When did they go?"

"At daybreak."

"They really went? All of them? Nobody stayed?"

"Nobody. The only live things left are chickens and pigs," answered Geminiano.

"Did they leave 'em? Well, I'm going to get me some. Let's all go get some," Amancio proposed, correcting himself.

There was no interest and he also gave up the idea.

"Yeah, that's right. Why should we, eh? We're free of them, that's enough. Leave the animals alone."

"If they stay there, they'll die," said Geminiano.

"No they won't. Chickens can take care of themselves in the rough. And pigs turn wild."

153

The church clock ground its gears and struck the hour slowly and incorrectly. The weight stone was already being lifted, the hands being reset. Time was being marked again, all of it, the good parts and the bad, just as it should be.

A Note About the Author

JOSÉ J. VEIGA was born in Corumbá, Goiás, Brazil, in 1915. While studying law at the Universidade do Brazil Law School in Rio de Janeiro, from which he took his degree in 1944, he worked as a radio announcer, 1938–41. From 1940 to early 1945 he was assistant editor, then editor, of *Revista do Serviço Público* published by the Brazilian Civil Service Commission. In 1945 he went to London to work in foreign-language broadcasting, and upon his return to Rio in 1950 he became first an editor for *O Globo* and later for *Tribuna da Imprensa,* both afternoon newspapers. Since 1952 he has been with the Brazilian *Reader's Digest,* where he is currently Editor for Condensed Books.

In 1958 Veiga's *Os Cavalinhos de Platiplanto* shared the Monteiro Lobato Short Story Prize with two other candidates, and in 1960 the same collection won the Fabio Prado Prize. He is also the author of *The Misplaced Machine and Other Stories* (1970).

A Note About the Author

A Note on the Type

THE TEXT of this book is set in Caledonia, a Linotype face designed by W. A. Dwiggins, the man responsible for so much that is good in contemporary book design and typography. Caledonia belongs to the family of printing types called "modern face" by printers—a term used to mark the change in style of type-letters that occurred about 1800. Caledonia borders on the general design of Scotch Modern but is more freely drawn than that letter.

The book was composed, printed, and bound by H. Wolff Book Mfg. Co., Inc., New York, N.Y. Typography and binding design by Edith McKeon Abbott.

A Note on the Type